THAT SUMMER IN ROME

THAT SUMMER IN ROME

LOUIS LORRAINE

CUTTING EDGE

ISBN-13: 978-1-962896-33-7

Published by
Cutting Edge Books
PO Box 8212
Calabasas, CA 91372
www.cuttingedgebooks.com

CHAPTER ONE

BRILLIANT October sunshine streamed into the office, causing Assistant Professor Claire Frazier to lift her head wistfully and gaze at the vivid scene outside. A crimson maple tree partially hid her view. Beyond the maple stood yellow oaks, several evergreens and a wide campus lawn. A small brown and white dog rolled in a pool of red leaves, scrambled to his feet, shook himself, then trotted off hopefully after a squirrel.

And now the sunshine had begun to remind her vividly of last winter in Rome, of the mornings spent in strolling around museums, cafés and art shops, of the afternoons in lazy cat-comfort sitting at tables in outdoor cafés or on the Spanish Steps, and of the nights—ah, the nights with Gino.

She sighed. She had only one big regret about her affair with the young Italian artist—she had had to leave Gino and Rome and return to college after her sabbatical year was over. What had made her begin the affair? Partly Gino's attractiveness, his charm, his zest for life. Partly her own frantic realization that she was thirty years old and had never known what it was to love.

But what she had had with Gino hadn't really been love. She saw that from the distance of several months and several thousand miles. Rather had it been a desire for love, a need for the pleasure and brightness of love, for love's reasonable facsimile because the real article was not available.

She smiled ruefully. There she was again, searching for explanatory words—acting like an English teacher, which she was.

1

Gino had teased her about the way she was always trying to explain in words, the way she had looked up things in that English-Italian dictionary she had carried around.

"Not everything is in that book," the artist had warned her, his eyes shining. "I tell you, Claire, my light, my love, you cannot find all you seek in that book."

"Good afternoon."

The deep voice made her start. She turned around in her chair. The new psychology professor, Wayne Kincaid, had come in and was standing before her.

"Am I disturbing you?" he said.

"No, of course not," she said pleasantly. Inwardly she was annoyed. He bothered her with his sarcastic remarks, his questions, his cross-examining of a person who might venture the least remark. She hadn't liked him since the first faculty meeting.

He sat down across from her. "Is this where your unruly pupils come to be scolded?" he asked, looking around her office. She had a feeling he was studying all the features of the office in an effort to analyze her character.

"This is a college, Mr. Kincaid," she said stiffly. "The students here are adults, or ought to be. You must be thinking in terms of high school."

He had taught four years in high school before obtaining his Ph.D. and this teaching post at Dexter College in Georgetown.

"I am vividly reminded," he said, "not of high school but of grade school students. Were you at the football game last Saturday?"

"Yes." She added reluctantly, "The students get restless sometimes. They have to blow off steam. I can understand—"

"Fine—then explain to me why a group of adults decides that an innocent game decision is so unfair that it warrants a riot in the stands and on the football field, the ripping apart of goal posts, the manhandling of several coaches who were foolish enough not to run for their lives."

She bit her lip. "I understand," she said with great restraint, "that there were several incidents last year that caused resentment to build up. I wasn't here so I don't think I could explain. If you're concerned, why don't you speak to Dean Carmichael?"

"Where were you last year?" he wanted to know. He was tall, he had dark-brown curly hair, he was a bachelor and—he was attractive. He probably thought he could ask any impertinent question he liked and that it would be all right

"On sabbatical leave. In Italy," she said.

"Oh." He crossed his legs. "And did you enjoy your stay?"

"Very much." She stood up, closed her books, put papers in her portfolio. She wouldn't get any work finished here, she thought. She might as well retreat to her apartment.

"You're not married, are you?" he said.

"No," she said shortly.

He examined her with calm interest. "And you're—what— thirty-five? Forty?"

"Thirty," she snapped. Then she could have cursed for having fallen into his trap.

"Thirty. And you grew up in the midwest. You probably have the Bible Belt philosophy about religion and sex. That causes more frustrated spinsters than any other set of misconceptions—"

"I'm not interested in your half-baked psychology!" Claire exclaimed, wanting to hit him as he sat there with his maddening detachment. Maybe she had felt frustrated enough to have an affair in Rome, but that was none of his business, none at all. "Now, I'm going to close up and leave," she said.

"I was thinking about what you said the other day," he said, making no motion to leave. "You remarked that a professor, in order to teach well, is necessarily somewhat emotionally involved with his students. Well, the more I thought about that, the more I realized your idea grows out of a lack of balanced love-relationships. You are trying to substitute these students for the husband and children you never had."

"And you're insane," she said angrily. She could feel the heavy flush rising in her cheeks. Her face was so fair that her flesh showed pink at the least embarrassment "I would feel the same if I were a man. A teacher is involved with his students. He studies them to decide what their needs are and how he can best meet those needs so that he can help the students become the best possible adults."

"You can't help them if you're too close. You have to practice a critical detachment. Analyze them, stand off and look at them. That's how—"

He broke off at the sound of a rumble of voices outside. Now, as Claire went to the window to close it before she left, she saw a crowd of students milling around near the tennis courts beyond the campus lawn. The students seemed to be scuffling in an ebb and flow. The crowd was moving slowly, pushed by an inexorable force, across the campus toward the Administration Building.

"What in the world—" Claire muttered.

Wayne Kincaid joined her at the window. "Another riot," he said calmly. "They had a rally this afternoon, didn't they? The president will have to clamp down. They're getting out of hand."

No use arguing with him, she thought. It only encouraged him and made him more combative.

"I think I'll go on home," said Claire. She closed the windows, locked them, waited impatiently at the door for him to leave, then closed and locked the door. She crooked the books with her left arm and took the portfolio in her right.

"I'll see you home," he said. "Where do you live?"

She was not interested in becoming involved with Professor Kincaid. "I have several errands to do," she said shortly. "Don't bother."

"That crowd sounds mean."

"They know me. They won't bother me. You're the new one," she said maliciously. "You had better run on home."

He raised his eyebrows. Her dislike seemed finally to have penetrated his thick skin. "All right," he said. "If I get trapped in the mob and they carry me off to the guillotine, I'll tell them, 'I'm a friend of your beloved Professor Frazier,' and I'm sure I'll be released."

"I wouldn't count on it," she said tartly, and went on to the mail boxes in the Treasurer's office.

She picked up her mail, stopped to talk to a secretary there and, when Claire emerged, Professor Kincaid had disappeared. She was relieved. She hoped he wouldn't come around any more. She distrusted anyone so prying and sarcastic.

She left the building to find that the crowd of students was milling around the doorways. The boys parted to let her pass, and she walked along the fringes of the crowd. Fighting and loud arguments seemed to be taking place in the center, but she paid little attention.

"Hi, Miss Frazier."

"Hi, Bob. Hi, Dan." She smiled at them and continued.

"Hi, Miss Frazier." It was Jerry Arnold, a senior and a football hero. She paused beside him as he stood at the edge of the crowd.

"Hi, Jerry. What's going on?" she asked.

"Oh, things got rough at the rally. The campus police were there because of last Saturday and the kids didn't like it. They tried to make the guards go away before the rally. So there was a fight. The guards brought a fire truck and hosed down the crowd. Made the kids mad."

Now she saw that many boys and girls were dripping wet, their clothes soaked, their hair hanging in limp strings and their faces flushed with anger.

"That was too bad," she said sympathetically. "I'm sorry it progressed so far." Claire saw another of her students in the crowd, Elsie Zeck. Elsie was an extremely shy girl who never spoke in class and who wrote rambling and passionate essays and poems she invariably turned in at every class session. Elsie was soaked, her plaid skirt limp, her cotton blouse clinging tightly to her rounded body. She was shivering in the cold autumn air.

"Elsie ought to go home and change. She'll catch cold" said Claire. "Elsie?" she called. The girl's shy gaze turned to Claire. Elsie stared with her slanted, oddly lovely green eyes. Then she smiled. "Elsie," the teacher urged, "you'd better go home. You're soaking wet."

The girl looked down at herself. "Wet?" she said. "Oh, goodness!"

The voices attracted the attention of several boys nearby. They turned around.

"You sure are, girl, and on you it looks good," one of the boys said suggestively.

Another boy laughed and plucked boldly at the wet blouse. "Why don't you take it off and be comfortable?"

Claire realized the boys could see right through the wet transparent material of the blouse and the thin bra underneath. The girl's breasts and nipples were clearly outlined. Elsie jerked away, embarrassed. "Let me alone," she said.

"We're just trying to help," said another fellow. They crowded around her, pushing her back with their hands and arms, closing in on her. The girl's head raised like a trapped animal's. The men were staring at her appraisingly, reaching out to touch her.

"No, don't. Let me alone, please. Go away."

"We're not hurting you. Give a cheer for Dexter. Lead us in a cheer. Come on, you'd make a gorgeous cheerleader."

Claire tried to shove a path through the boys. "Let me through," she said. "Let that girl alone." But, teasingly, they barred her way.

"Give us a cheer. Come on." One boy caught Elsie's arms, forced her to raise them in a mock cheer. "One-two—three—four—who are we for? Dexter! Dexter! Come on—you know it." The men stared even more concentratedly, as the girl's body moved.

Elsie closed her eyes and screamed—a thin frightened sound. Claire twisted around to Jerry Arnold.

"She's scared and upset," Claire said. "I've got to get her out of there. They don't realize she's terrified."

He nodded, and used his hips and shoulders to force his way through the small tight crowd of boys around Elsie. The rest of the mob paid no attention to this minor event in the corner near the building.

"Come on, now, let me past. Easy there—" Jerry fended off a rough elbow. The boy turned, his resentment ready to break out

"Oh—Jerry. What are you doing?" he asked.

"Let me get that girl out—"

The boy backed away reluctantly. Claire followed closely behind Jerry who slipped past the shuffling, sweaty boys teasing Elsie. At the center of the tight ring Elsie swayed, her eyes closed, in a trance of fear. Claire caught her in her arms, pushed away the boy trying to make her cheer.

"Let her go. You're scaring her," Claire said.

The boy held on a moment longer, then finally let Elsie go. The girl's arms dropped like the loose arms of a puppet, and she sagged in Claire's grasp.

Claire was really alarmed. "I'll have to get her to the clinic," she told Jerry.

The other boys drifted away. A couple of them stared curiously as Claire and Jerry helped the faint girl across the campus to the college clinic. She seemed scarcely able to walk, and then she began to cry, quietly.

The nurse at the clinic took one look at Elsie and called the doctor. Between them they maneuvered her upstairs and lowered her gently to the bed. Claire waited uneasily in the downstairs room.

She said to Jerry, "Those boys really scared her. She's so shy. She didn't realize how attractive she appeared, how she stirred them up."

"That was too bad, Miss Frazier." Jerry sat down beside her on the wooden bench, his blue eyes earnest. "That's the trouble with a mob like that They don't know what they're doing, and somebody gets hurt. Usually an innocent person."

"I know." She put her hand impulsively on his big rough hands. "Thanks for helping Jerry. I couldn't have gotten her out alone."

He blushed, the color visible under the dark tan of his cheeks. His blond short hair was bleached unevenly by sunstreaks. He moved awkwardly on the bench. "That's okay. I was glad to help you. I guess I'd do anything you asked me to."

She felt abruptly uncomfortable before the worship in his eyes. She knew some of the boys developed crushes on her. She hadn't realized Jerry felt that way.

The nurse reappeared. "The girl's better now," she said. "No injuries, but the doctor wants to keep her here a couple days. She has had quite a shock."

Claire said, "Let me know if there's anything I can do."

"Why don't you stop in tomorrow afternoon?" the nurse suggested. "She'll probably want someone to talk to."

"I'll do that," Claire promised, and left the building with a feeling of relief, Jerry beside her.

When Claire and Jerry emerged from the clinic, they saw the students milling along the streets toward town.

"I'd better take you home, Miss Frazier," said Jerry. "Some of those guys are acting silly."

"Thank you," she said gratefully. "What's the matter with them, Jerry?" she asked as they turned toward her street. "They rarely acted like this before."

"I was talking to some kids at home this summer," he said. "They told me it's the same at their colleges. Everybody's restless. They don't know why. Somebody says something, and the kids flare up. One of the boys went down to Fort Lauderdale. Man, that was really wild, he said. I guess the older folks are taking over down there."

"Older?"

"Yeah. I mean older women, prostitutes, older men out for kicks. He saw one guy sporting a college cap. Said the guy was fifty if he was a day, and had a big pouch belly. What a laugh."

They skirted a crowd of boys who were talking loudly, excitedly. They gave Jerry and Claire a long slow stare, but Jerry steered Claire past without incident.

She had never before felt afraid on the Dexter campus. She had thought that she knew everyone, that everyone knew her and that no one would harm her. It was odd to realize, she thought, that in a mob nobody was safe. Mob hysteria was a crazy thing.

She was relieved to arrive at the door of her apartment on the second floor above a five-and-ten-cent store.

"Come on in, Jerry," she said impulsively.

He came in, closed the door after him. She had violated her own rule—not to invite any men students singly to her apartment. But Jerry Arnold was a nice boy. Besides, she didn't want to be alone, not just yet.

"This is swell," he said, standing near the door and looking around.

Claire was a rather tall woman, five feet eight in her stocking feet, but Jerry dwarfed her. He was at least six feet two, she judged, and the loose football sweater made him look bulky.

"All those books," he said. "Have you read them all?"

"Not all," she said. She ran her hand affectionately over a row in the bookcase as she passed. "Many, though. And I'm always buying more. Would you like some coffee?"

"I sure would. But it would be a bother," he added. He hadn't moved from where he stood near the door.

"No bother. I was going to make some for me. I'm cold." She shivered. "That wind was keen." And, she added silently to herself, an unnameable fear had made her feel chilled.

She moved a small drop-leaf table out from the wall with Jerry's aid.

"Let me," he said, adjusting one drop-leaf. "Do you want the other side up?"

"No. That's big enough." She went out to the kitchen to make coffee. He followed her like an overgrown puppy, eager to help.

"Do you eat all your meals here?" he wanted to know.

"Most of them. I got tired of restaurant food long ago."

"How long have you been a teacher?"

"Seven years. If you count last year, when I had a leave of absence."

"I missed you," he said simply. "I was going to take Modern Novel, but I didn't when I found out old Lawson was giving it."

She smiled. "You flatter me," she said lightly. "Professor Lawson is a much better teacher than I am."

"Have you read *Lady Chatterley's Lover?*" he wanted to know.

She wasn't sure she wanted to discuss that book with him. "Yes, I read it once."

"Is it literature?"

"Some people say so. Yes, I guess so."

"Then why can't students discuss it in class?"

It took her a while to veer him away from that subject They had coffee, sitting at the small table. He was awkward, his long legs shuffling under the table, as he tried to get comfortable.

Abruptly she wondered what Professor Wayne Kincaid would have said if he had seen them. He and his remarks about frustrated spinsters.

"Did you meet lots of people in Italy?" Jerry said.

"Oh, yes, quite a few."

"Artists? Bohemians?"

"Yes. There are lots of artists in Rome."

"Did you like them? Or did they seem queer? Were they perverts?"

She jumped. The things that college boys talked about. "Oh, some were perverts, I suppose. The ones I knew were—ah—heterosexual."

"I'd like to go to. Europe some time," said Jerry.

Claire was glad the perverts had been dropped. "I hope you can, Jerry."

"Before I settle down in Dad's business," said Jerry, "I'd really like to go to Europe. You know, wander around and really see everything and meet people and get to know them."

"And the girls too, I expect," she teased lightly.

"Yeah." He didn't blush. "I think a fellow ought to know something about women before he gets married. Don't you?"

The question could be booby-trapped, Claire thought She circled it warily. "How do you mean?"

"I mean, a marriage ought to last a long time. Maybe a lifetime. Some marriages do. And if a fellow looks around and meets different women and gets to know the kind he likes, really likes, I mean, then he ought to know what kind of girl to marry. Shouldn't he?"

"Yes, I expect so."

"Why haven't you gotten married?"

She choked on the coffee. She coughed and coughed to clear her throat. He leaned over and pounded her back with rough efficiency.

"All right now?"

"Fine. Fine," she muttered.

"Why haven't you gotten married?"

She had had a moment to think. "I haven't met the right man. Sometimes one doesn't for a long time."

He stared at her with critical blue eyes. "But you're very beautiful. I should think a man would have married you by this time. He should have convinced you he was the right man."

"How about some more coffee?" She stood up. "I can make more."

"No, thanks. No more."

He stood up too and helped carry the dishes back to the kitchen. "I hope you aren't mad because I asked all those questions," he said.

It was impossible to be angry with him. She smiled at him. "No, of course I'm not."

"You are beautiful. In class sometimes I forget what you're saying because I have to stare at you. Your face is so pretty, and your eyes—they're green—and sometimes they look yellow-green, like a cat's."

She moved her head, uncomfortable under his stare. "You're very flattering." She tried to brush by him to return to the living room. He put out his arm swiftly and blocked her path.

"Sometimes when you were talking in class," he said, his hand boldly on her waist, "I would look at your mouth and wish I could close it and make you stop talking—like this."

She knew what was coming, but she was paralyzed. She stood still as a frightened bird as he drew her against his body. She felt his rough jersey sweater against her face before he put his hand behind her head and tipped it back. She stared up at him, at the blue eyes coming closer, dark blue eyes, intent, determined. Then she saw his mouth, big and full-lipped, the lips parted.

His mouth touched hers, experimentally. The youthful body pressed arrogantly hard. Her mind was swept back to Rome, to Gino, the night on the rooftop at the pensione where, so sure, so confident that she would give in, he had first kissed her.

Kincaid had said she was a frustrated spinster.

Jerry's young body was eager, ardent. His mouth was hot, the open lips wet on hers. Her body remembered nights of passion, her hips throbbed impatiently after months of denial.

She tried to pull away. His legs, in a slow dance of desire, moved after hers. He backed her to a cupboard, held her motionless while he kissed her again, while one hand held her head and another her waist, his lithe hips twisting against her thighs.

She sighed, and circled her arms about his neck. Her waist curved to his hand, her breasts crushed against his chest. She had known passion, and she wanted it again. She was starved for the touch of a man's body, the entrance of a man's hot flesh.

In a few moments he drew her, fluidly, into the bedroom where his swift eager hands undressed her. She thought, "How does he know how to do this?"

Then she lay naked across the bed, waiting, aching, watching him. He pulled off his clothes. She was surprised at his body. He was thinner in the main than she had expected, but his shoulders were wide, his chest sturdy, his waist and hips narrow, his legs long and straight. And the hair on his chest and thighs entranced her.

It had been a long time. Too long, she thought. When he came over to her, her hands raised greedily to clasp his back. He was ready, eager, anxious for the meeting. Like a swift summer storm he took her, hurting her a little, pushing impatiently to the heights, drowning her in soft rain.

She hadn't meant to let him go so far, but it was finished, and he lay in limp triumph over her startled body. Her hands clutched helplessly.

He propped himself up in a few minutes, his legs tangled with hers. He kissed her face, her lips, his dark blue eyes pleased, softened.

"Again," he said, not asking. Taking.

"Jerry—wait—please—" she gasped, as he moved. But already it was too late.

Again he stormed at her, won home. This time he lingered, kissed her, caressed her breasts with big rough hands. He was big in her, bigger than Gino, filling her, making her realize her helplessness and fragility.

He kissed her breasts, teased the nipples to hard taut rosebuds, then took them in his mouth. He rubbed his big body on her softness, increasing the pressure on her hips until the friction made her restless. She wiggled her thighs to free them. He lifted up slightly, let her swing herself. She felt him watching her as she moved, as she swung wildly, as her pleasure increased. Then her eyes closed, her body rhythm beating sharply against his.

She had fastened her blond hair up high, in the severe upsweep that made her look more like a teacher. Now she felt his hands busy in her hair, pulling it, ripping the braids apart, until the hair tumbled down over her shoulders.

"Lovely," he whispered. "Lovely—my lovely—"

His face pressed down in the rich blond mass. She heard his heavy breathing. She wanted to push him away, because she was coming, she could feel herself coming high and hard and wild. At the same time she wanted to grip him tight, wrestle with him, force him to please her.

She groaned, struck at his chest futilely. He was heavy on her. He pulled back, pushed forward again and yet again.

"Oh," she cried. "Darling—darling—"

The sweetness, the wild convulsive sweetness that Gino had taught her to know was here again. Her body crumpled with pleasure as Jerry climaxed, hard and pulsing, with her.

When she opened her eyes, she blinked at the rays of sunlight streaming from the windows. Sunlight—the sun—Gino, she thought. No, it was Jerry. This was not Rome.

But her lover was here, demanding, triumphant, his hand on her breast, wanting more.

CHAPTER TWO

CLAIRE was scarcely able to crawl out of bed the next day. Jerry had stayed till after two in the morning, and she was exhausted.

Her first class was a blur. She wasn't sure afterwards what she had said. But the class members had been sleepy as usual, and she doubted that anyone had noticed anything unusual.

She felt rather guilty about the session with Jerry. She must realize that she was very vulnerable now, and be cautious. Since she had discovered how sweet a lover's embrace could be, she found it extremely difficult to resist a virile approach. Her only sure defense was to avoid dangerous situations.

But she had enjoyed Jerry—his rough sure handling of her body, his confident attacks, his hips holding her down helplessly as he finished. And he knew how to give pleasure as well as take it. Yet he was only twentyone, a kid, she thought, surreptitiously stretching her aching body. What would he be at thirty? Wow, she mentally exclaimed.

She had no nine-thirty class, so she went off campus to a nearby drugstore for a cup of black coffee. That helped. Jerry was in her ten-thirty class, and she didn't want him to realize she had been enervated by their session.

Claire meant to be very cool and poised with Jerry from now on. He needn't think she was a conquest he could handle as he pleased. During the ten-thirty class she avoided his blue gaze, called on other students, and was generally brisk, efficient and business-like. Jerry didn't say a word to her during class.

Afterwards she detained three girls to discuss their essays. Jerry hesitated, then left. Claire was both relieved and disappointed.

After lunch she had a two o'clock class, then several interviews. When the last student had departed, Claire filled her brief case with papers to grade and locked her office. She didn't intend to linger and chance a visit from Jerry. And she was in no mood for Kincaid's sardonic remarks.

She had nearly gone past the clinic on her way home when she suddenly remembered Elsie Zeck. The girl hadn't been in class, and Claire had promised the nurse to stop in and see how the young girl was getting along.

Several students were waiting in the reception room, and eyed Claire curiously. She spoke to the nurse.

"Is Elsie Zeck still here?"

The nurse looked up from her folder of case histories and smiled. "Oh, hello, Miss Frazier. Yes, she is. Im so glad you stopped by. She has been asking if you were going to come see her."

"How is she?"

"Better. The doctor will probably release her tonight or tomorrow. She wasn't hurt, really. Just shocked and hysterical."

Claire mounted the stairs to the room at the end of the hallway. She tapped lightly.

"Elsie? It's Miss Frazier."

"Come in."

Elzie Zeck was sitting up in the high hospital bed, propped against two fat pillows. She wore an attractive green bedjacket, that revealed a pale green nylon nightgown. The green set off the emerald of her slanted eyes and the black of her gleaming curly hair.

"Oh, I'm so glad you came, Miss Frazier. I've been wanting to thank you."

Claire sat down in a chair beside the bed. "It's quite all right, Elsie. How do you feel?"

"Fine. I—I wanted to ask—" "Yes?"

The girl hesitated, blushing and stammering. "I'm so ashamed—the way I looked. And all those b-boys—staring — How d-did I look, Miss Frazier? Why did they stare at me like that?"

Claire tried to be tactful. "You were soaked from the hosing. And your blouse was thin. They could see your ah—arms—"

"And my chest?" asked Elsie, anxiously.

Claire suppressed a grin. "Well," she said, "not clearly. Only the outline—" Claire wasn't a good liar, but Elsie seemed so distressed that the teacher thought the effort justified.

"I can't face them again, ever!" said Elsie, tears in her eyes. "I'm so embarrassed. What do they think of me?"

"They think you're a darned attractive girl," said Claire firmly. "They went too far in teasing you, but you shouldn't be scared of them. They meant no harm. They were excited. I expect all it will mean is you'll be asked for a lot more dates."

"Do—do you really think so?" asked Elsie. "They—they don't think I'm terrible?"

"Quite the contrary. They think you're very pretty."

"Oh." She leaned back against the pillows and thought about that. She seemed more calm, and Claire was pleased.

Heavy footsteps sounded on the stairs, in the hall. "May I come in?" asked Jerry Arnold.

Claire's first frantic feeling was that she was trapped. She wanted to run. Jerry loomed over her. He was so tall, so confident. He put his big hand lightly on her shoulder, his fingers pressing significantly.

"Sit still, Miss Frazier," he said. "I'll get another chair. How do you feel, Elsie?"

Elsie's green eyes followed him with surprise and adoration. "Oh—I'm fine, just fine!"

He hooked a chair, pulled it near the bed, twisted it around and sat down on it, his arms folded across its back as he leaned casually forward. He seemed to fill the room with his masculinity, his calm assurance.

"I'm sure glad to hear that," he said. "The fellows were mighty upset when they realized you were in the clinic. They said to tell you they didn't mean any harm."

"I know. I mean, Miss Frazier just said that too."

Her eyes watched his every casual movement. Claire might as well be a hundred miles away, the teacher realized with amusement. After all, Jerry Arnold was a football and basketball star, a senior, a Big Man on Campus. Elsie was probably overwhelmed.

"I told the guys I'd come and see how you were getting along. And if you weren't improving, I said I'd beat them all up. So it's up to you—shall I whip them for you?"

"Oh, no!" said Elsie, responding to his grin with a shy adoring smile. "Oh, don't do that. I'm getting along fine. The doctor said I can go back to the dorm maybe tonight or tomorrow."

"That's great. If any of the guys bother you after this, just tell them Jerry Arnold will get after them. Okay?"

"Okay," she sighed.

Jerry turned to Claire. "Elsie is in one of your classes, isn't she, Miss Frazier?"

"Yes, she is," said Claire, trying nervously to avoid his eyes. Elsie stared dreamily at Jerry.

But Jerry was looking at Claire, his caressing gaze on her shoulders, her breasts. It was as though he were touching her with his bold hands, preparing her for another virile assault from his big tough body. She resented that the gaze of a mere boy could make her shiver and stiffen.

Gino had similarly affected her. After the first night in his arms, she had only to meet him at a cafe, sit beside him, and know how he was looking at her, and she would feel her body melting with desire. Then Gino would touch her hand, whisper, "Come, Claire," and she would go with him anywhere he wanted.

Why was she so weak? She had always thought of herself as a strong, proud, independent woman. Gino had blasted her defenses to bits in one evening. They had dined by candlelight. He had sat so close to her that his leg rubbed insinuatingly against hers. They had had wine—yellow, sparkling, bubbly glasses of wine until her head had swum. Walking back to her pensione, she had stumbled on the cobblestoned street. Gino had caught her, had drawn her back into a dark doorway, had pulled her weak body against his ardent one and had kissed her till she was deaf and blind and drowning in passion. They had gone to his room, a large bare attic room, the walls covered with his paintings, the bed spare and Spartan. There Gino had taught her how frail she really was, how weak, how innocent.

Claire shivered in remembered ecstasy and then returned to the present with a start. Jerry was talking to Elsie about football, explaining the plays patiently. He was a nice boy, thought Claire. He was very young, even younger than Gino. She was foolish to worry about her reactions to Jerry. Jerry was only a boy. She could handle him easily. Last night had been an interlude, an incident that would not be repeated.

Another girl tapped along the hallway, paused at the door. "Hello?" she said tentatively.

"Harriet. Come in," said Elsie, sitting up. Her bedjacket fell back. Jerry stared hard at the lovely young bust revealed by the thin gown.

Claire was amused. She stood up.

"This is Harriet Middleton, my roommate," Elsie introduced the new girl. "Harriet—Miss Frazier. And Jerry Arnold," she added, with a gentle sigh.

The girl's eyes widened. "Jerry Arnold!" she exclaimed. Harriet glanced at Claire. "Oh, it was terribly nice of you to rescue Elsie," she said to the football star. "She was simply scared to death."

Jerry was standing also, awkward before Harriet's obvious admiration. "That's okay. I'm glad she's getting along fine," he said.

"I must go," said Claire hastily, taking advantage of the situation. "I'm so glad you're fine, Elsie. I hope I'll see you in class tomorrow."

Elsie smiled at her. "I'm so grateful, Miss Frazier."

"That's all right. Goodbye." Claire backed out of the room, keeping a wary eye on Jerry. But her measures were in vain. Jerry followed her out, echoing her farewells.

"Goodbye, Elsie," he said. "Take care."

"Goodbye, Jerry. Thank you very much for coming."

Jerry travelled down the hall beside Claire, his hand proprietarily on her elbow. "I'll walk you home," he said.

"That isn't necessary," she said, hastily, hating the crazy feeling that was sweeping through her at the touch of his warm fingers.

"I want to see you again," he said in a low growl.

"We mustn't—no—" Claire tried to say.

The nurse was at the bottom of the steps. "Thanks so much for coming, both of you. How do you think she looks?"

"Fine," said Jerry. "I think she's fine." He didn't release his taut grip on Claire's elbow.

"I think she'll be all right," said Claire.

"Good. That's fine. The doctor is coming back at seven. I think he may release her tonight."

Jerry's grip on Claire's arm was possessively tight as they walked down the street silently.

It was as though both knew what would happen, as though the same thoughts were in both minds. Claire felt helpless, her body restless and desirous. Her defenses had been overcome before Jerry had made any attempts to take her …

Jerry drew her closer as they walked along. He slowed his pace so she could keep up with his long legs. He said, easily, as though making polite conversation, "I can't get you out of my mind. I hadn't any more than left you last night when I wanted you again."

"Jerry," Claire said, uneasily, glancing down the street No one was near enough to hear.

He laughed softly. "Did you get any sleep after I left?"

"Of course. I slept hard. I was tired," she snapped, unthinkingly.

He chuckled again. "You're sweet. You're wonderful. I can hardly wait—" He moved his hand casually up her arm until the back of his big hand pressed hard against her breast. She couldn't pull away without a public struggle.

"Jerry, this can't go on and on."

"Why not?"

"I didn't intend to let you at all—"

"But it happened. Why shouldn't we do what we please?"

His hand pressing against her breast, his low voice coaxing, her own resistance at an ebb, she stopped pretending she didn't want him as much as he wanted her. Once inside her apartment, Jerry took her in his arms.

His mouth pressed hotly on her, his sturdy arms enclosed her. Once again she felt the urgent warmth of his strong body. He drew her down to the couch.

"Wait—Jerry—not so—"

But he couldn't, wouldn't wait. His hands bared her as swiftly as Gino's had. She adjusted herself under his youthful body, her hands gripped the rough wool of his sweater, she closed her eyes as she felt him lunge.

He took her so fast she gasped for breath. He plunged recklessly, deeply. Within moments, he lay across her, spent, his head on her breast. She caught a glimpse of his blond, boyish face, the eyes closed, the mouth slightly open. He was content, satisfied.

He sat up, moved her legs casually so he could sit beside her. She swung her feet to the floor and stood up, feeling cross and rumpled. She pulled her slip and skirt down over her hips, and she was not a little flattered by his intimate gaze.

She had begun to be aroused. If he left now, she would be angry and frustrated.

"I'll change to something comfortable," she said.

He followed her to the bedroom, watched as she stripped and then put on a full-length blue nylon quilted robe. She unfastened her hair, brushed it deliberately, let it hang loose to her shoulders.

By the time she turned back to him, he wanted her again, fast He put his hands on her waist, kissed her. She let him feel her warmth, then drew away slowly.

"How about some coffee?" she said. She wanted to punish him for using her like that, leaving her when he was satisfied. This next time he would make love to her first before he could take her.

"Why not—do this—come on—" He tried to urge her to the bed.

"Not now. Later," she said provocatively. She smiled at him over her shoulder.

He followed her to the kitchen. He could dominate her with his body, but not with his mind, of that she was sure. While she fixed coffee, she chatted lightly about school matters, aware of his impatience. He sat down at the table but couldn't sit quietly—he reached out to touch her knee as she drank coffee. She let him move the robe aside, let him fondle her knees and thighs.

"Claire—may I call you Claire?"

"Here, yes. But not on campus," she warned.

"All right. Listen, Claire." His fingers pressed urgently on her thigh. "Couldn't we go to bed now?"

"Soon now." She made him wait longer. "Don't you have football practice today?"

"No. I'm supposed to be resting. I twisted my foot yesterday."

"This isn't exactly resting."

"If we went to bed, it would be!"

She laughed softly at his sparkling blue eyes. "Do you like sports? Or are they a way of getting through college?"

He moved impatiently. "Oh, they're okay. I'm not grim about them. Dad doesn't feel I should go in for pro ball; I don't want to either. It's a rough life. And he wants me to carry on the family business. I work in the plant during summers."

"And this is your senior year."

"Yeah." His fingers kneaded the flesh of her inner thigh coaxingly. She felt heat rising rapidly in her body. Deliberately she finished her coffee.

"Claire—" he said desperately.

She stood up, stretched, let the robe "fall open. "All right, Jerry. Let's go to bed."

But he had to touch her first, to put his big hand at her breast. He drew her down on his knees, shoving the table aside. His left arm held her, his right hand drew the robe away from her body so he could look at her. His hand swept in a heavy caress from her shoulder to her breast, and then from her waist to her thigh. She leaned back, watching him with slumbrous eyes as he bent his head to kiss her with savage nuzzlings.

"Jerry. Don't hurt." She ruffled his short hair with her hands, her long fingers clever on his head and neck.

"I want to taste you, bite you," he said, his voice muffled as he kissed her thigh.

She smiled down at the body crouched over her knees. Then she pulled up the sweater at his waist and put the flat of her hand on his back, held it there so the warmth would penetrate.

A shudder coursed through him. He lifted his head, looked at her with eyes that had turned dark. His face was taut.

"Claire. Now. Let's go to bed."

She stood up, let him draw her to the bedroom, serenely confident that this time she would have what she wanted. She let him push her down on the bed. When he would have followed her down, she protested.

"Not yet, Jerry. You undress too."

He flung off his clothes, then sprawled naked beside her. She laid her hand on the hairy chest of the boy almost a man. It pleased her to make him do what she wanted.

"Do it slowly this time, Jerry," she coaxed. "I want to feel it too."

"Whatever you want," he said.

"Then let me—oh, you know. You're so big I wont crush you."

He smiled, pleased and intrigued. She guessed that he had never made love that way.

"Sure. You go ahead." He lay flat while she climbed on him. She flung off the robe, then crouched on his hips. She was hotly desirous now, her passions fully aroused by his playing with her body.

She bent lower, her hips seeking his. She found him, pressed slowly, trembling with excitement as she played the aggressor role. Gino had taught her this also. He had taught her a great deal last winter.

Jerry watched, fascinated, as she caressed him with her hands, kissed his chest and shoulders, pressed closer, harder, moved frantically as her desires built higher. She felt it coming, cried out, crouched down—and collapsed on his body as sweet convulsions beat through her.

Jerry rubbed her back with his hands as she lay across him, their legs still tangled. His hands were big and hard, the fingers calloused. She liked their roughness, the masculinity of the young body under hers.

She rolled off, lay sprawled out beside him. He bent over her, touched her. "Hey. I liked that. That was different."

She smiled lazily. She was satisfied.

"Let's try some other way," said Jerry eagerly. "Turn over."

Her brain was too bemused to realize what he meant. She let him roll her over on her stomach. As he caressed her back, his eager hot mouth on her shoulders and waist, she sprawled contentedly. She liked to be kissed, to be handled by caressing hands, to feel a man's stomach and legs pressing on her.

She was lulled to submission as Jerry moved about awkwardly on her. Oh, well, she thought, she had what she wanted. He could play all he wished.

"Jerry," she cried suddenly as his next action dismayed her. She tried to rear up but his weight held her down.

"Hold still. I want to—"

"No, I—no!"

"Come on, Claire. Let me try this. I've been wanting to do this to a woman."

He was already in possession. It was too late. She wiggled to avoid his further attack, trying to close her legs. He laughed in excitement.

"Do that again!"

She wiggled again to please him. She moaned, then. She lay helpless as he went on and on. She felt the hard bar of his arm across her back, holding her. His hips were big, his body hot above hers...

When it was finished, he held her in his hard young arms. "You liked it too, didn't you, Claire?"

She moved her head. "No. No."

"You did. I could feel how you did."

She sighed. She had not wanted to be dominated, even physically. But it had been thrilling to be made to lie submissive and accept his attacks. And after all, he was only a boy.

"Yes, I did like it."

He laughed in delight. "I thought you did." He kissed her shoulder, his hand claiming her big breast. "Let's try—uh—I mean, I read a book once—"

She could have groaned. The trouble with kids nowadays was they read too many books. She tried to calm him down, coax him to lie quietly with her. But he was aroused and passionate, his youthful body eager and ardent and untiring.

He stayed all night, and they got little sleep. He wanted to run the full gauntlet of love. Claire aroused also, was satisfied by her virile lover again and again. He was a good lover, almost as imaginative as Gino.

For the next several weeks Jerry visited her as often as he could get away from his studies and football. He complained whenever the team played a game away from home, and he rushed back to her with renewed vigor.

Claire tried to keep his visits to a minimum. But Jerry was reckless, his young body eager to taste again and again the new pleasure it was discovering. And the woman found it impossible to refuse, her own body demanding satisfaction after the years of denial.

CHAPTER THREE

THE faculty meeting had been going on for two hours, and the room was warm. Professor Wayne Kincaid found his attention wandering from the discussion of several problem students. He suppressed a yawn, swallowed hard and sat up straight in the large armchair.

He realized after a while that his gaze was focused on a blond head two rows in front. Claire Frazier. He had noticed her at once this fall when she returned to the campus. He had sought her out, tried to talk to her, but then in the pressure of many duties he had forgotten her again.

He shifted sideways in the chair so that he could see her more fully—her creamy skin, the faint pink flush on the cheekbones, the good nose, an interesting full mouth. He had noticed her mouth before, he remembered. Her lips were full and soft, like a pulpy flower. She was thirty years old, unmarried, and she had spent last winter in Italy.

His eyes narrowed. She was an attractive woman, probably unawakened. It might be interesting to date her. She had been cold to him. That had put him off. But maybe she was not cold underneath. That mouth might be a clue to a more passionate woman.

After the faculty meeting broke up, Wayne managed to be standing at Claire's side as she turned to leave the room.

"Hello, Claire," he said. "What do you think about the Ellis boy?"

Her large green eyes gazed at him, then narrowed like a cat's. He was interested to see how her eyes reflected her thoughts. He knew before she spoke that she would rebuff him.

"He is in capable hands," said Claire. "I'm sure Dean Carmichael can manage."

Wayne persisted, walking beside her out the door. "Do you still think a professor should take such a personal interest in his students?"

"My ideas do not change so rapidly," she said coldly. "I have thought that for some years. Please excuse me. I want to speak to Professor Lawson."

She left him without a backward glance. Wayne was amused and intrigued. She was trying very hard to be indifferent to him. She disliked him now. Perhaps she was secretly afraid of men.

The next day he came to her classroom late in the afternoon. The November sun shone through in crimson rays. Most of the leaves were gone from the trees, and the black branches were silhouetted against the western sky.

"Hello Claire," he said cheerfully.

She started, and glanced up from reading papers. She gave him a look of pure dislike before she could mask her feelings. There were dark rings under her eyes, and her shoulders drooped as she bent over the desk, her chin propped on her hand.

"Hello, Professor Kincaid," she said wearily. What do you want?"

"You look tired. You've been working too hard," he said, rather concerned.

She seemed to take his concern for sarcasm, and blushed. "You are surprised that I work at all?" she asked curtly.

"No. I mean it That's quite a stack of papers to read. Do you assign papers very often?"

"At least once a week for the essay course. Not so often for the lit. courses."

He whistled. "No wonder Dexter College has a reputation for turning out good writers. But it's rough on the teachers."

She eyed him warily, as though she were not quite sure how to take this. He followed up rapidly.

"What I came to ask is, do you like chamber music? There's a very good quartet in Columbus, and I have a couple tickets. Next Saturday evening."

"Oh," she said. "A quartet? What are they playing?"

"All Beethoven. Maybe that's a bit heavy for your tastes."

She was reluctantly interested. He was amused again at the struggle she was going through. She wanted to go, but not with him.

"The late Beethoven quartets," he added, "Pretty esoteric."

"Oh, I'd love to go," she said. "I haven't heard good chamber music since last winter in Rome. I used to go all the time to the Sistina—they had a concert every week, often chamber music. And the Accademia—" She stopped abruptly.

Italy had evidently been a tremendous experience for her, he thought. He determined to follow up that lead.

"The concert is at eight-thirty Saturday night I'll pick you up at five-thirty, then we can have dinner in Columbus."

"All right. Fine. Thank you."

He checked around and found there was a good Italian restaurant in town that featured candlelight, wine and good Italian food. He made reservations.

Claire was obviously delighted with the place. And Wayne decided, looking across the candlelit table at her, that she was well worth the effort he had made. She wore an emerald-green silk dress cut low across creamy smooth shoulders, sleeveless, the bodice tightly outlining full breasts. She wore long slender dangling gold earrings that accented the slim long throat. Her hair, sleek and golden in the light, was swept back and wrapped around her head in a suave line. Her expressive green eyes sparkled, the candle flames reflected in the pupils.

"This is perfectly lovely," she said. "However did you find it? It's so out of the way, I've never heard of it before."

"Like a bit of old Italy, isn't it?" said Wayne, pleased.

"Yes. Have you ever been to Italy?"

"No. I hope to get there. Most of my time since college has been devoted to saving money for the university, then getting my Ph.D."

She made a rueful grimace. "That's what I should have done. I'd be a full professor like you. Instead I spent my money recklessly on books, records and travel."

"I bet you don't regret it, though."

"No. I don't, really. Italy was beyond my happiest dreams. The colors—the sunlight on marble, the pale sea-shell colorings of Giotto's bell tower in Florence, the magnificent golden doors, all the mosaics and frescoes and paintings—" She shook her head, and the candlelight glittered on her gold earrings. "Whenever I try to describe it, I sound like a raving idiot."

He encouraged her to talk, and to drink the golden-white wine chilled to perfection and to remember the romantic beauty of Italy. They were late getting to the concert, and people scowled at them as they stumbled into the semi-darkness of the small concert hall.

The music was good. Wayne came close to forgetting the purpose of this date in his satisfaction with the music. The strings sang in the delightful precision of the movements, the sounds deeply eloquent.

When they left the hall, he took Claire's arm and found she was trembling. The music had evidently affected her, excited her. That was something else to remember and use.

Driving back to the college town, he tried to think of the best way to approach her. She was silent, staring at the dark country road ahead of them. He decided to be blunt.

"Look, Claire, we've had a good time together. We have the same tastes."

She jerked. He could feel the start she gave. "Oh, do we?"

"Yes," he said blithely. "And you're a damned attractive woman. Let's go to my place and finish the night in style. It's been quite a while since I've met anyone as pretty as you."

"Thank you so much for your flattery, Professor Kincaid. But I'm not in the mood to pay for my dinner with a quick roll in the hay. Pick yourself a green country girl."

He had goofed up for sure. He could have kicked himself. She was a romantic, and he had tried a brash modern "you're as smart as I am about this" approach. Hell. He should have stuck to the candlelight and wine and music routine. He could have sworn she was ready to be seduced.

That was it. Seduction. She wanted a romance with all the gold and pink trimmings. Maybe her year in Italy hadn't quite educated her.

He kissed her goodnight at the door, but she turned her head so the kiss was only a quick brush of her cheek. It took him another two weeks to persuade her to date him again. This time he had a complete set-up planned.

He asked her to dinner at his apartment to hear some new records of Beethoven and Schumann chamber music, and to try some wine he thought she might like. He had candles on the table, and he lit them for the meal, after which he turned out the lights in the room.

"I'm a romantic," he said, with little regard for truth. "I think good wine should be drunk to music and candlelight."

Claire smiled. "I like that too." She lifted the wine glass in her long fingers, turned it so the wine bubbles sparkled. "Pretty," she murmured, as though her thoughts were far away.

She was wearing a pale beige wool dress, a thin gold chain around her neck from which depended a small gold medallion at the hollow of her throat. Wayne watched the medallion move as her pulse throbbed. He was becoming excited himself from the warmth of the room, the intimacy of the candlelit dinner, the heat of the wine in his throat. He had better go slow on the wine if he wanted to keep his head and complete her seduction.

He urged her to talk about Italy. "I'm planning to go there myself one of these years. Where should I go first?"

"Northern Italy first. I'd take a ship and get off at Genoa. It's a lovely old port city. Be sure to see the home of Columbus. And have coffee in the galleria."

"What's the galleria?"

"It's a large glass-ceilinged shopping lane. Milan has a lovely one, Naples, too. Naples' galleria is famous. An American wrote a book about it. I don't remember his name. Funny. My head is spinning."

"Have some more wine," he said, and filled her glass again. "Genoa first, and then where?"

"Milano," she said dreamily. "And Lake Como. Don't miss the lakes. You really mustn't miss the lakes. Then Venice. Oh, Venice is so beautiful. You're in another world, a world of the fifteenth century. All gold and ruby and the sunlight on blue water." She finished her glass and he filled it again.

"And then?" he prompted softly. He wasn't going to make the mistake of being blunt and crude. But he was beginning to want her. He smoothed his hand slowly over her bare arm. She shivered. He left his hand on her wrist. Her pulse was beating more rapidly.

"Then—Florence. Florence is sixteenth and seventeenth century. Michelangelo. And the street shrines. You walk along an old cobblestoned street and look up, and there on the wall is an exquisite painting covered with glass, with fresh flowers laid on a little stand before it. Or a Madonna and Child by Della Robbia, the most tender blues and whites. I liked to stand in the morning in front of the golden doors and watch how the sunlight glanced off the gold."

"And then—" he prompted. He put his hand carefully on her waist and rubbed caressingly.

"Then—Rome. Most glorious of all. The colors are incredible. And the music. And at night I would stand at the top of the Spanish Steps and look out over Rome. My Rome. Shining and beautiful, the lights—the lights—"

She paused and put her head down on her hand, her elbow propped on the table. "Dizzy," she said. "I'm getting dizzy."

The music on the record player was going on and on. A candle gutted and flared bright, then flickered out. Wayne slid his hand around her, held her in his arm, moved her face with his other hand until she was resting her head against his shoulder. He pressed his mouth against her cheek, her ear, her throat. Then he kissed the open red mouth, a long slow hot kiss with open lips.

He felt her shaking. He kissed her again. She stirred, tried to pull away. He kissed her closed eyelids, murmured, "Don't leave me. Don't leave—"

Slowly he drew her to her feet, held her in his arms as he kissed her. Slowly he drew her over to the wide couch. Another candle gutted and went out. The room was in semi-darkness.

She stumbled against the edge of the couch. He pressed her down, lifted her legs and laid them out straight. He casually pulled up her dress above her knees before lying down with her.

She stirred, murmured a protest as she felt his body. He put his arm under her head and kissed her mouth, long and ardently. All the time his hand stroked over her, over the big breasts that rose and fell more rapidly to her quickened breathing, over the slim waist, over the full hips. He pulled the dress higher, higher, to her waist.

She lay lax under his caressing. Her eyes were closed, her arms flung up above her head. With careful touch so as not to startle her, he bared her lower body. He could see her only dimly in the darkened room, but what he saw excited him. Her thighs were creamy white, full, the hips rounded.

She was not struggling. Slowly he stroked her, fondling, squeezing. She lay limp, but her breathing was rapid. When he bent over her, her arms moved. Her hands came up and her arms circled him. He felt her hands on his back against his shirt. She was gripping him with hard fingers.

He could wait no longer. He thrust with a powerful movement. She was a big woman. He had noticed that she was tall, only a few inches shorter than he was. Her hips moved convulsively. She was trembling now, her hands grabbing at him. He had not felt such a surge of passion for years. He had left women out of his life, except for the most casual bedding, for a long time. He hadn't wanted to become involved emotionally. Now this woman, he found, was a very satisfying one.

She was big and she held him tight between her arms and her long legs. He moved on her, enjoying the rich pleasure of her body, the smooth softness giving way to his demands.

Blood drummed in his ears. The wine was blurring his mind. He felt hot, impatient, furious for release. He moved faster, eagerly seeking pleasure. In the midst of his release he felt the convulsions gripping her. Her body quivered in his grasp as he flooded her with passion.

He was dazed with joy as he lay beside her again. What a woman she was, so soft, so receptive, so responsive. He held her in his arms, caressed her body eagerly until he was ready again.

He leaped with her in a frantic search for pleasure. She let him do whatever he wanted, moving with limp submission as he directed. At the peak, she clutched him with her body. This was no naive innocent spinster, he judged. Here was a full rich awakened woman, responding with passion to a man's determined seduction.

He took her again, then again, in the eagerness after long denial. He was impatient with his body when he had to wait a while after one of the embraces before he could take her again. He longed for the strength of a Jove, to lay with a woman as many times as he wished, to stop the movements of the earth and make one night the length of three.

But he was mortal, and grew weary. And so he fell asleep, his hand on the warm thighs of the woman who had pleased him so much.

He woke abruptly to find Claire sitting up beside him, staring at him with amazement and anger. She had found the lamp beside the couch and turned it on.

"What did you do to me?" she cried foolishly.

"Plenty," he sighed, trying to urge her to lie down again.

"Oh—you bastard, I could kill you."

She pushed him away and struggled to rise from the couch. She was beautiful in her confusion and her fury. He watched her as she pulled on her clothes. Her hair was down over her shoulders.

"I must have been drunk," she groaned. "To let you —I could kill you."

"I thought from the way you reacted that you were enjoying it," he said, smiling.

The way she glared at him he knew she was really angry. "I didn't know what I was doing—you got me drunk on purpose."

"I wanted to find out what kind of a woman you are. And I sure found out."

She struck him. The blow glanced across his cheek, but it was hard enough to rock him. He caught her hand as she raised it to strike again.

"Take it easy, Claire. I could rape you if I wanted. Do you want me to?"

She pulled her hand away, regained control of herself with an intense effort. She went to get her coat

"I'll drive you home," said Wayne. He got his coat and swung it on, yawning.

"I'd rather walk," she said coldly.

"At three-thirty in the morning? I'll drive you."

She finally allowed him to drive her home. He said at her door, casually, "When can I see you again?"

"Never!" she blazed.

"Don't kid me," said Wayne harshly. "You may have been drunk, but you knew what I was doing to you. And you liked it."

She slammed the door in his face. He shrugged, returned to the car and drove home. At his apartment he thought he would go right off to sleep. But he was unable to.

Claire was no naive, timid soul. She was an experienced woman. Why did she deny she had enjoyed the night? Surely she had known something of what had been happening.

He would have to have her again. No woman that marvelous should be allowed to pretend she was a frustrated nervous spinster. Wayne smiled in the darkness, his body stretching with remembered pleasure, his hands moving on the blankets. Claire. What a beautiful woman. The next time he would undress her completely so he could see all of her. How many times had he taken her? He hadn't counted. And sometimes one embrace had flowed into the next

Claire. He turned in the bed and lay on his stomach, thinking of her soft body moving convulsively under his. Claire.

CHAPTER FOUR

THE life of Elsie Zeck changed abruptly after her watersoaking at the football rally. When, after her discharge from the clinic, she finally moved back to the dorm, men began to telephone her, to seek her out on the campus, to carry her books to and from classes, to look at her sideways with speculative glances.

And Dan Evans called her for a date. Dan was a senior. It was rumored that his family had loads of money. He drove a flashy red convertible and dated any girl he pleased.

The first time Elsie turned him down. She was scared to death.

"Oh, no, I couldn't—"

"Why not?" Dan asked, his voice soft and wooing.

Elsie's hand on the telephone was damp. She bit her lower lip as she looked from the phone booth at the girls in the hall. What would they think if they knew Dan Evans was calling her?

"I—I don't know you," she stammered.

He laughed softly. She shifted the phone to her other hand and wiped her left hand on her housecoat.

"How do you expect to know me if you won't go out with me?"

"I—I don't know."

She put him off, and he became more eager and excited. He called her again the next evening.

"If you turn him down again," said her roommate, "I personally will have you locked up for a nut. You're crazy if you don't date him."

Elsie gingerly approached the phone. "H-hello," she said.

"Hello, Elsie. This is Dan."

"Oh, hello."

"Have you thought it over about dating me? How about tomorrow night?"

She closed her eyes and swallowed to clear her throat If only this were Jerry Arnold calling her, how happy she would be. Maybe Jerry would notice her more if he knew other men were interested in her. He hadn't paid any attention until the scene on campus.

"All—all right. I'd like to go."

"Good! I'll pick you up at eight."

"I—I don't know what to wear," she said foolishly.

"I thought we'd go dancing."

"Oh. Okay. I'll wear a formal. Shall I?"

"I'd like that"

They talked for a while, and Elsie found it wasn't so hard to talk to Dan as she had feared. He liked to tease her and kid her.

Word soon spread around the dorm that Elsie Zeck had a date with Dan Evans. Her status shot up. One girl offered to lend her a lucky bracelet. Another offered advice on how to handle men like Dan.

"He'll take you out in the car after the dance and park somewhere. Now, seriously, Elsie, don't let him do any more than kiss you and neck a little. If he starts petting, you're sunk."

Elsie wanted to ask the girl how sunk she had been on her dates with Dan. But she didn't. She just listened carefully.

On Saturday night Dan came for her promptly at eight, bringing her a delicate green orchid—"to match your eyes," he said.

Elsie was so nervous her hands shook when she pinned the flower on the shoulder of her white net formal. She felt a terrible innocent.

But Dan was nice. They went dancing at a hotel in town, and filled in the time between dances with light gay chatter about campus doings.

She felt funny, the way he held her later in the evening. For a while they would dance with his hand at her shoulder blades. Then slowly his hand would slide down her back to her waist, and for a few moments in the dance he would hold her so hard against his body that she could scarcely move. She felt scalded with hot embarrassment at the way he imprinted his lower body on hers. Was he doing this deliberately? Did he realize—yes, of course he did, she decided.

After the dance he drove out into the country where they parked in a dark lane. He put his arm up on the seat behind her.

"You're a cute kid, Elsie," he said.

She wished again she were with Jerry Arnold. What a crazy world this was. All the girls in the dorm envied her for being out with Dan, but she would rather have been with Jerry. Why hadn't Jerry called her for a date? She had seen him staring at her chest when he had visited her at the clinic. She touched her breasts furtively in the darkness. Men must like to look at breasts. Why hadn't Jerry called? Did he think she was too young for him, to immature, too inexperienced?

How did a girl acquire experience enough to attract a wonderful man like Jerry Arnold?

Dan moved his hand to touch her shoulder casually. She could feel his hand through her coat She looked up at Dan in the darkness, troubled. Should she let him kiss her? She wasn't serious about Dan. Was it wrong to let him kiss her?

Dan took the problem out of her hands. His arm moved around her, his other hand came up to her face. He bent over, brushed his mouth against her cheek, then kissed her mouth, slowly, firmly. She smelled the lotion on his face, the tobacco smoke from his cigarettes.

Elsie sat rigid as Dan kissed her again. She liked to be kissed. It was exciting. She felt a pleasant shiver along her spine.

"Don't you like me?" Dan whispered.

"Yes."

"Then kiss me."

His mouth moved on her lips. Absorbed, she made her mouth move with his and she forgot to be rigid. Her body relaxed. Even when his hand moved down from her throat to her breasts, she stayed quietly in his arms and let him caress her. She liked it, even though this was Dan and not Jerry.

Dan's big hand cupped a breast through the net of her formal. She remembered what the girl had said, not to let Dan pet her. But Elsie liked being petted. And how else could she get experience?

Dan's kisses became harder and more exciting. He mussed her up, kissing her throat, then pulling down the stiff fabric of her formal to kiss the tops of her breasts. He nuzzled against her, both his arms around her tightly, pushing her back against the seat.

Her stomach felt peculiar, and her legs were rubbery. She put her hands on his head to push him away.

"Don't, Dan. Don't."

He lifted his head. "You're sweet, Elsie. Let me kiss you. I won't hurt you."

She let him kiss her some more. When he started to put his hands under the short skirts of her formal, she pushed him firmly away.

"No, Dan, no more. Take me back to the dorm."

He sat up with a sigh. "You're a tease. You let me go far, then you make me stop."

He didn't seem angry. He took her home and asked her for a date the next Saturday. She agreed to go.

The next Tuesday, Dan saw her coming out of a class and asked her if she would like a coke.

"Yes, I'd love it."

Elsie enjoyed the looks on the faces of girls as she walked by them with Dan Evans carrying her books.

At the drug store they sat down in a booth. Dan managed to touch her knees with his as he sat down across from her. She pretended not to notice, her eyes down, looking at the menu.

"Coke with lemon," she said, when he asked what she wanted.

"Hi, Dan. Hi, Elsie."

"Oh, hi there, Jerry. Don't you have football practice now?"

Elsie could have jumped up and screamed. Jerry Arnold had appeared out of nowhere and stood beside their booth.

"I'm supposed to be there right this minute. How are you, Elsie?"

"F-fine."

"You're looking great." Jerry's gaze lingered frankly at her chest, on the swell of the green sweater where her coat was open. Deliberately she pushed back her coat, then took it off slowly. Both men were staring at her. It felt wonderful to have men staring at her, admiring her, wanting to touch her.

Elsie wished she could think of something to say or do that would make Jerry notice her, really notice her, and ask her for a date.

"Well, got to go now," said Jerry. "See you around."

He turned and lounged out. Their cokes arrived. Elsie sipped hers. One of these days Jerry would notice her. He would look at her, and stay, and touch her under the table the way Dan was doing now.

If only she were more experienced. Well, there was only one way to acquire the experience she needed.

The following Saturday she wore a new black format She had bought it especially for the occasion. It was black net over layers of black crinoline, and the skirt was daringly short and full. Dan whistled when he saw her, his gaze admiring.

They didn't stay very long at the hotel on this occasion. They danced for only a short while. Dan held her tight in the dancing, and she let him mold her body to his.

They went out in the car afterwards to a dark lane and parked. Elsie unfastened her coat and pushed it back. She knew what she intended to do tonight.

Dan put his arms around her right away. "Elsie, you're terrific, you're so cute," he whispered.

She leaned her head back on his arm and lifted her face for his kiss. She kissed him back with parted lips. He got excited right away, and began kissing her harder. She let him.

When he kissed her throat, then the flesh above her breasts, she put her hands on his head and tickled his neck. He growled something and kissed her more fiercely.

He put one hand tentatively on the black net over her breasts. When she didn't protest, he pulled the stiff net folds down slowly, until her breasts were free of covering. She gave a little gasp as she felt them bared. But she had vowed that tonight she wasn't going to stop Dan. She wanted experience, and he was the man who could give her that.

He cupped one breast in his hand. His thumb moved her nipple until it became hard and pointed. He kept brushing it with his thumb. The delicate sensitive flesh of her breasts responded to his touch.

He kissed her breasts, holding the nipples in his mouth. She felt her whole body melting in heat as he went on nuzzling at her. He put his hand under the black net skirts under the stiff petticoats of the crinoline. She didn't stop him, even when she felt his hand on her inner thighs.

"Elsie, are you just teasing? I want you sol" She heard his broken whisper, and a wave of sheer triumph went through her. It was wonderful to have a man want her so much.

She didn't stop him. His hand on her soft flesh became bolder, more demanding. Her breathing quickened as he touched her in sensitive places. His head was pressed against her breasts, but both of them were thinking only of her legs. She knew that was what he was thinking about because he didn't kiss her; he only held his mouth tightly pressed, unmovingly against her breast, while his hand moved with tantalizing and controlled impatience, exploring her slowly.

Then he shifted. She was chilled, disappointed as he sat up. Was he going to stop? She didn't want him to stop. She wanted him to go on and on, and teach her what she was so curious about.

"Elsie," he said. "This is your first time, isn't it?"

So he knew. He knew she was innocent. "Yes."

"You want it, don't you? You want me to love you?"

"Yes." She swallowed nervously.

"Then let's he down in the back. It will be easier for you."

She let him guide her to the back seat. He closed the doors. She lay down. He drew up her skirts, pulled off her panties. She was scared, but she wanted to go on. She saw him in the dimness, pulling down his trousers. Then his hands touched her again. He kissed her breasts, caressed her, put his hands on her cold thighs and warmed her skillfully.

"It will hurt you at first, just a little," he murmured. "You won't mind it after a few moments. It will feel so good. You wait and see. Don't be afraid."

He lay down with her. She became panicky, then, but he soothed her and whispered to her how sweet she was and how she would like it. He rubbed his hands on her, and rubbed his warm hips on her bare ones. She felt the heat burning through her once more, and when he started pressing against her body she let him.

He was slow and careful. He was a nice guy, thought Elsie gratefully.

"Put your arms around me," he said. "Bend your knees. Like that. Yes."

His head was on her bare breasts, kissing them. Her body felt one long fire. He was pushing himself at her. She tried to back away.

"Don't move away. Move toward me," he said.

She couldn't. It was starting to hurt

"Come on, sweet," he said. "Now."

She wasn't big enough. He was too big—he—oh, no, no—There was a bright blaze of pain, flashing through her body. She screamed and tried to wrench away. It was too late. He was past the barrier.

Then the pain was gone, leaving only a dull ache. There was a weight inside her. Dan was gripping her body, urging himself further.

She writhed. Her brain was blurred. It hurt, but now she wanted it. She wanted it fiercely. The pressure, the tightness, the heaviness, even the pain felt—so good. She was beginning to belong to the whole human race, to become a member of something tremendous.

She felt strange and dizzy, then, hot and limp. Dan moved faster. It was odd to feel a man's hips bare on hers, his muscular thighs moving within hers, scraping against her softness.

Then Dan lay inert on her as he held her tight with his arms and body. She shivered violently. She felt Dan shivering. Then he rolled off and sat up.

His hand stroked her lower body, the quivering legs. He was whispering something tender. He didn't have to soothe her. She was happy. Now she knew. She knew why men wanted women. She knew what they did to women. She knew what it was all about.

When Dan bent down over her again, her arms came up and welcomed him. He was a nice guy. He had been good to her, gentle in his initiation of her. She was grateful.

CHAPTER FIVE

THE more Claire thought about what the obnoxious, detestable Professor Wayne Kincaid had done to her, the angrier she became. She hated him. He had gotten her drunk and had raped her. Then he had had the colossal gall and gigantic ego to inform her that she had enjoyed the experience and had participated in it willingly.

It made her burn with helpless rage to think of him. She had been out cold. She was sure of that. Of course, she amended, she did remember a great deal of what had happened, and if she had been out cold she wouldn't have remembered, would she? But she had been numbed and paralyzed with the wine, that was for sure.

Wayne Kincaid was a stinker. He was a bastard, a rapist, a seducer, a bastard. Claire whispered the words viciously. Bastard fit him best. He was not a fit teacher. She would not be surprised if he would receive his just due and be kicked out of the college.

If she had known what he had been up to, she would have kicked him in the teeth.

He had the gall to ask her for another date. She stared at him in cold fury.

"I should say not," she said. "Are you out of you mind? Do you think I would ever go out with you again?"

"Of course you will," he replied with infuriating assurance. You enjoyed it as much as I did. You need more experience, but you aren't the inept spinster I thought you were. How about Saturday night?"

She couldn't think of any words blistering enough to wreck his superior attitude. She turned on her heel and left him. Back at her apartment she thought of several crushing replies, but it was much too late to deliver them.

He had been laughing at her. There had been a twinkle in his dark eyes, a suggestion of a smirk on his lips. And the way he had stared at her body as though he owned it. She got furiously angry all over again.

Wayne sat beside her at the next faculty meeting. He kept leaning over and whispering remarks in her ear. Rebuffs meant nothing to him. He was insufferably vain.

After the meeting he said, "How about Saturday night?"

She glared at him. "I'm busy," she snapped.

"How about Sunday?"

"I'm busy then, too."

"My, you're a busy girl," he drawled, a quirk at the side of his mouth. "You're going to have to crowd me into your schedule. I'm not going to be left out."

She walked away from him again. She was shocked to find she was shaking, her hands trembling. Why did she let him affect her like this? He was a bastard. She would forget him, ignore him.

He came to her classroom at four the next day. She was readying to leave stuffing papers into her portfolio. He walked in and closed the door. In spite of herself she felt panicky.

"Hi, Claire. Say, that's a lot of homework."

"I'm busy," she said feebly.

"What about Saturday night? I have tickets for—"

"I don't care if you have tickets for the moon. Get out and let me alone!"

"Darling, you sound violent," he said mildly, coming closer to her desk.

"Don't call me darling!"

He put his hands on her shoulders as she sat at her desk. He rubbed his hands caressingly over her upper arms, back to her throat. Then he tipped back her head against his jacket and bent down.

"Don't," she commanded.

He kissed her mouth. She jerked away, almost fell over in her chair.

"Look out, darling," he said.

"Let me alone."

"But you can be so sweet. You have a marvelous body, you know."

She flung away from him and stood up. Her eyes blurred with tears of rage at his teasing.

"I told you to let me alone. Do you want me to report you to the authorities?" She backed away as he followed her. "Let me alone—I'll scream."

"I'm betting you won't."

He backed her into a corner. He was laughing. It was her final humiliation. She stiffened as he put his hands slowly on her waist pushed her into the corner with his body and legs, held her there motionless. She had meant to scream, or to bite him, or kick or— His mouth came down on hers, his lips half-opened. The heat of his body seemed to paralyze her as the wine had paralyzed her that night in his apartment.

She endured his kiss, holding her body as stiffly as possible. His mouth moved on hers. His tongue insinuated itself between her lips, explored the roof of her mouth, touched her tongue, pushed aggressively. A fiery twinge snaked from her head to her heels, weakening her spine, her hips, her legs. She crumpled against him, wanting his body, wanting his masculine attack to subdue her entirely.

He let her go, let her move away from the wall. "You do like me," he said blandly. "Now let's set the date for Saturday." He was smiling, arrogant, confident.

And she had been about to give in. In a blind fury at herself she struck him, her open palm slapping hard against his cheek. A red streak marred his face.

He stared at her, the smile dying away. Then swift as lightning he pulled her toward him. For a moment she thought he was going to kiss her again. Instead he whirled her around, bent her over, and spanked her twice, hard, on her buttocks.

Then he sat her down hard on the chair. "You're a spoiled brat," he said, and walked out.

Her hips stung. He was a tough bully. He was a bastard.

Claire felt like crying. She had never hated anyone so much in her life. She had never felt so helpless, so infuriated. She had been able to control Gino and Jerry also. They had never treated her as Wayne Kincaid treated her. He was a mean, devilish—

Control, she thought. She sat up slowly, staring blankly at the walls of her classroom. Control. She had been able to keep Gino and Jerry under control. Was that why she had had affairs with much younger men? Had they been successful with her sexually because they had been able to dominate her only physically?

Kincaid tried to dominate her mentally as well. He had seduced her in a clever way, forcing her to connect him with Italy and Gino, whether he realized what he had done or not. But Kincaid himself was quite different from Gino. Kincaid was adult. She was afraid of him, and the emotional domination he might achieve over her.

Was she afraid of a man her own age, a mature sophisticated male? Gino had been young, gentle. His body had dominated her, but always she had been able to keep her mind apart, concealed from Gino's knowledge. She had made the effort to prevent him from knowing all her thoughts. She had deceived him sometimes, and he had not discovered it.

Jerry was like Gino, a big husky kid only beginning to learn how to control a woman's emotions. He could never dominate Claire. Nothing lasting could grow out of their romance. And they both knew it.

She shook her head violently. She didn't want to believe the facts she was beginning to perceive. She hated Wayne Kincaid.

She liked Jerry Arnold. That was all. She mustn't get a complex. She mustn't start psychoanalyzing herself. That would lead to trouble.

There was a big football game scheduled for the Saturday before Thanksgiving. Dexter College was playing their traditional rival, and the rival had won the past three years. This year there was some hope of reversing the trend. Dexter had been winning most of its games this year.

On Saturday afternoon, Claire turned on her radio in the apartment to the college station. Jerry had been quite excited about the game, so she thought she would tune in while she graded papers. She didn't feel she could take the time to go over to the football field, and it wouldn't be nearly so tiresome as trying to get through the crowds.

It was an exciting game. The score was tied at the half. At the beginning of the fourth quarter the score was tied again. Claire stopped trying to grade papers and gave her entire attention to the game.

"It's first down for Dexter, and goal to go," yelled the student announcer. "There's the signal"—the Dexter team is really hot today! There goes Bud Mayhew! The ball is in the air—oh, oh—no—no—yes! Jerry Arnold caught it! Jerry got it! He got it—he's away—he straightarmed the—there—there he goes! Over the line! Over the line! It's a touchdown. Wow!"

Claire grinned in excited sympathy as the crowd screamed in the background. The point after touchdown was lost, but the game was won. Dexter held, the minutes ran out. Jerry had won the game.

She snapped off the radio. Jerry was quite a boy, she thought proudly, before she turned back her attention to grading her papers.

She was startled when Jerry arrived at the apartment an hour later.

"Jerry! What in the world—"

He came in and closed the door behind him. He had a dark green bruise high on his cheekbone, but a beaming grin on his face.

"Did you hear the game?"

"Yes. Congratulations—that was a wonderful play."

"Thanks." He came over and took her in his arms. He kissed her hard, and she kissed him back affectionately.

"You must be tired. And that bruise—I'll get an ice pack."

"No." He caught her arm as she started for the kitchen. "I don't want anything but you. I want to celebrate."

"Celebrate?" she gasped.

"Yes. Don't you think that game was worth celebrating?

"Sure, Jerry. It was wonderful—the campus must be going crazy. Why don't you go out and join the kids?"

His eyes flashed angrily. "Let the kids celebrate any way they damn please! I know how I want to celebrate! He pulled her close, knocked the breath out of her with his violence, and began kissing her cheeks, her throat.

"But Jerry!" she sputtered. "But—Jerry—Jerry—"

He pulled her with him to the bedroom. He was in no mood to be put off. Jerry Arnold did have some power over her, Claire conceded, as she let him undress her with swift hands. She didn't have any wish to stop him now.

She lay back on the bed, naked, her body warm and eager for his. She watched him flinging off his clothes with rough impatience. His hair was still wet from his shower, the bruise on his cheek was fresh and raw, she saw other bruises on his chest, on his long legs.

He was naked also. He came over to the bed, bent over her, staring at her with dark stormy eyes. She gazed up at him. She had been thinking of Jerry as a boy. Now he didn't seem like a boy at all. Her breath caught in her throat as he touched her breasts with possessive hands, moved to lie beside her.

"Claire. You're so beautiful. Claire." His lips followed his hands. She felt his mouth moving over her breasts, teasing the soft nipples till they rose up in points for him to catch in his mouth; his tongue played deftly with each rosy point, titillating the sensitive flesh. She stiffened in voluptuous desire.

His hands were becoming too clever. He was learning too well how to stroke her body, where the sensitive places were, how to caress her until she held up her arms and stirred her hips impatiently.

A boy? He was becoming a man too quickly, and she was learning to be afraid of him and his power over her. This must stop, she thought because pretty soon she wouldn't be able to control Jerry any longer.

If only he would take her fast and leave her unsatisfied. Then she could dislike him and feel superior to him. If only he hadn't learned her so well, learned how to linger over her, smooth her flesh, kiss her breasts, rouse her, make her wait.

She resented that Jerry knew how to build her up. She tried to think of other things, to keep herself from surrendering. But Jerry's lean body was crowding out all other thoughts. His mouth was open on her breasts; he would draw the heart out of her.

He must have felt her surrender. He lunged at her, and she fell back before him, opening weakly, letting him seek and find her softest secret place.

Her quivering began, she held to him, she cried out to him. "Jerry—darling—Jerry—sweet—take me fast. Hard. Love me."

"I love you," Jerry whispered. "I love you, Claire."

She realized, with a sense of keen dismay, what he had said. Oh, she hadn't meant to let him love her. This was only an affair. He was only a boy.

"I love you," he whispered, his head on her breast. They were tightly held together, his weight was heavy, her body encompassed him. She felt tenderness, joy, compassion, and also a hot impatient desire.

"Jerry—Jerry—" She pulled demandingly at him as he moved away. He smiled, thrusting full at her. It touched off fireworks inside her. Convulsions swept her body. She was helpless in their grip, her hips trembling. Jerry lay across her limp body.

From somewhere she heard bells. Were they inside her head? As she gradually recovered, her hands stroking Jerry's soft blond hair, she realized the sounds were the bells on the college campus. Kids were shouting, yelling.

"Jerry, they're celebrating the game."

"Yes," he said, lifting his head from her swollen breasts. "So am I." He smiled down at her, possessively, bent and kissed her mouth, a slow forceful kiss. She closed her eyes under the domination. No, she would not let him control her. This was Jerry. He was only a boy.

But how sweet a boy, she thought later, as he made love to her again. How sweet, how knowing, in the way he gave her pleasure.

It would be hard to give up Jerry. This must be broken off, this must be stopped before he really came to love her as he thought he did already.

But she would miss him a great deal. The affair should never have continued so long. She would long for him many nights, many empty nights.

Professor Wayne Kincaid was furiously angry with Claire. Why couldn't a woman be honest? he thought Some people called women complex. No complexity at all, said Wayne. Claire was just plain dishonest. She refused to recognize her own emotions.

Claire had yielded to him that night, yielded beautifully, gloriously. Maybe she had had a lot of wine to drink, but she hadn't been out cold, not by a long shot. Her body had responded to his, her arms and legs had held him tight His back had been bruised for a week from the frantic clutching of her strong urging fingers.

Why couldn't a woman be truthful? Why did she demand soft lights and music for her seduction, instead of admitting she liked a guy and going off to bed with him whenever they could arrange it?

And when Wayne had kissed her in her classroom, he had felt her body sag, surrendering to him. A moment later she had struck him. He muttered a curse. He had always known women were inconsistent and unpredictable, but Claire was an intelligent well-educated woman. One would think she would know herself well enough to be honest.

She had refused to date him again. Why? She had enjoyed their session, he could swear to that. A woman couldn't fake her reactions, not for the number of times he had taken her.

Wayne shifted in his chair, stared broodingly at the record player. He was thinking too much about Claire. He ought to go out with other women, find a girl who was everything he wanted, marry her, start a family. He was thirty-two years old. He had his Ph.D., a good job, a good salary, and he was tired of living alone. A man needed a woman, not just for occasional hot nights, but for always. Any night he wanted, waking, turning to the woman beside him, touching her, waking her. That was the way it ought to be. A woman for a lifetime.

He stretched, leaned his head against the plush back of the chair. Claire. What kind of a wife would she be? He had enjoyed talking to her. She was wonderful in love-making. Could she cook? He grinned, absently. With a woman stacked like Claire who cared? But she probably could cook. She lived alone, ate meals in her apartment. It stood to reason she could cook or she would be eating in restaurants all the time.

When he had calmed down, he decided his approach to Claire had been wrong. She wanted romance. She wasn't sure of his intentions. He wasn't sure of his intentions, either. The best thing to do, since he couldn't edge Claire out of his mind or become interested in another woman, was to date her again, learn to know her, figure out if she was the kind of woman he wanted to marry.

It was easier for the psychology professor to decide on the right method than it was for him to carry it out. Claire continued to refuse him, coldly, absolutely. She scarcely spoke to him. She avoided sitting beside him at meetings, she avoided him at socials and receptions.

That night in his apartment Claire had shown him she was not a frustrated spinster. Wayne finally decided she was an independent bachelor girl who would have to be convinced that marriage to the right man was better than any amount of freedom.

Wayne liked to classify women. He thought it made them easier to handle. He had approached Claire with the wrong tactics, thinking of her as a frustrated woman who needed to be initiated boldly into the pleasures of sex. As a bachelor girl, she would have to be handled in an altogether different manner.

He couldn't seem to get anywhere with her, though, no matter what technique he used. He must have scared her quite thoroughly that wine-and-candlelight night. He didn't believe that she was afraid of him so much as she was afraid of her own responses to him.

By the middle of December he had made no progress. Christmas vacation was coming up. It would be a shame to waste two weeks.

He went to Claire's classroom at four o'clock of a cold winter afternoon. The overhead electric lights were on, and the reflection gleamed in her blond hair as she bent over the papers on her desk. With a small fraction of his mind he paid tribute to her hardworking qualities. She really knocked herself out to be a good teacher. But when he looked at her, he could only sigh, "What a waste —a gorgeous woman like that to spend her time in a career."

Claire Frazier looked up from her papers, and a small frown line appeared between the dark blond eyebrows. Her greenish cat eyes narrowed, flared again. She was on guard against him, thought the psychologist

Wayne walked over in front of her desk and seated himself on a one-armed student chair before Claire.

"Teacher, may I ask a question?"

Her mouth twitched as though she might smile. "What is your question?"

He raised his voice slightly in a mock treble. "My daddy is paying my bills and my mommy says I should go to college. But I'm not learning anything. What should I do, teacher?"

Claire laughed out loud, her green eyes shining. "Don't tell me you're getting those questions."

"Cross my heart, so help me. It's incredible. Why do the little morons think they are in college? Don't they know by this time? I feel like kicking them out of college and making daddy pay the bills for a student who is keen to learn but doesn't have the money to come."

"Rank socialism," she mocked lightly. "Besides, I feel if a student begins to question why he is here, there is some hope for him. He may even start to learn."

"Claire Frazier, the optimist of Dexter College."

"I can't help being optimistic. It seems to me that students now are so much keener, so much more knowledgeable than when I went to college. They know more, they care more. We don't have the stagnant flat atmosphere we used to have. I could almost smell the decay of ideas. Now, the kids are waking up. They can do something, they can change the world, at least a small part of the world. What they do counts, and they know it."

He grinned, teasingly. "I like it when you get up on a soapbox."

She flushed, the animation dying out of her face, a guarded wary expression masking her eyes. "You like to devil people to find out what makes them tick," she accused.

"Yes, I do," he admitted frankly. "I like people, even when they make me mad. They interest me. I want to know more about them. But people won't be honest. They aren't truthful about their feelings and emotions. Take you, for instance."

He could see her stiffen, her shoulders turning rigid.

"I can't be sure you say what you mean," he went on, keeping a curious eye on her shoulders. It was interesting how Claire betrayed herself with her green eyes and her expressive body. He enjoyed forcing her to react to his thoughts. "The night you stayed at my apartment, you knew what I was doing to you. You weren't passive. You responded."

"You keep saying that but it's not true—I was drunk."

"If that is so, I wish you would let me get you drunk again," he sighed.

She was deeply flushed, angry, afraid. "I'm not going out with you again."

"You are afraid of me, then," he accused.

"I am not."

"Then you ought to go out with me. How about Saturday night?"

"No. But that doesn't mean I'm afraid. It simply means I don't want to be bothered."

"And I bother you? How much? Do you dream about me?" he teased. At least she was talking to him.

"No." She stood up. "I can't get any work done here. I might as well leave."

He stood also. "What are you doing at Christmas time?" he asked bluntly. "Look. I want to know you better. I think we could be great friends, if nothing more. Why don't we go somewhere together and find out?"

"Absolutely not." she said curtly. She gathered up papers and stuffed them into her portfolio.

"Why not? It could be fun. And no one would know, if that's what is worrying you. I'm not about to kiss and tell."

"Get this straight. I don't want to go out with you for one evening. I certainly don't want to go on a trip with you. You certainly are the most arrogant, most conceited—"

"What are you doing at Christmas time?"

"I'm going away—by myself," she snapped viciously. She closed the portfolio and fastened it.

"Where? Florida? It would be great to—"

"No. Not Florida."

"How about New Orleans?"

"No, I'm going to New York, to see some plays, and get away from people I know. Now, let me alone."

"I could come to New York with you. You don't want to go to plays all by yourself. And think what fun we could have, some great fights—"

Her mouth curled a little, but she wouldn't smile. She held open the classroom door and flipped the light switch. He walked out reluctantly.

She walked down the hall a step ahead of him, her back straight and rigid. It was fun to fight with her.

Why not go to New York? Wayne grinned as he thought of that. He could go to New York by himself. She had no monopoly on New York. They could run into each other casually. She couldn't object to that.

If he could only find out where she was staying. He watched as she went into the treasurer's office. She talked for several minutes to the secretary there. They seemed to be pretty friendly. His eyes narrowed.

The next afternoon he went to the treasurer's office and asked the girl to cash a check for him.

"By the way, Sue, do you ever get to New York?" "No. I never have gone there." She smiled at him.

"I'm trying to get someone to recommend a good hotel. I haven't been to New York for several years. Do any of the profs go regularly?"

"Professor Slater does. But he always stays up near Columbia."

"Oh. That's too far. I wanted to be near the theaters."

"Professor Lawson likes the New Prince Hotel," she suggested. "I know he recommended it to Miss Frazier."

His heart leaped. With an effort he kept his face from showing his glee. "The New Prince Hotel. Do you know the address?"

She gave it to him.

"That's right in the theater district. Great," he said, writing it down. "Thanks a lot, Sue."

"You're welcome," she said kindly. Sue was the kind of woman who enjoyed being helpful. And how very helpful she had been. Wayne whistled blithely all the way back to his bachelor apartment, happy in spite of a couple inches of slushy snow, several days of grey skies and the prospect of grading a couple hundred exam papers.

Now he had something to look forward to during the Christmas holidays. Christmas in New York—with beautiful and passionate Claire Frazier. What man could wish for more?

CHAPTER SIX

CLAIRE had been considering leaving the campus for the holidays. Jerry was becoming too serious and demanding. She had never in the world meant to let their affair go on so long.

With Gino the problem had been simple. There had been a built-in time schedule because, when her sabbatical leave was finished, she had had to quit Rome and Gino. That was that. They had both understood the situation. No hard feelings, only regret at parting. Perhaps Gino had felt, as she had, a slight relief at knowing there would be a definite clean break to end their affair.

It was hard, thought Claire, to have an affair, to enjoy someone's lovemaking, to bask in the warmth of exciting admiration and adoration, and then have to feel the affair breaking, the attention waning, the uneasiness setting in as one partner or the other lost interest. How much better to have a limit at which the affair could gracefully come to an end. There would be no shattering of ego, no smashing of pride and self-confidence.

She was beginning to tire of Jerry. She still enjoyed their embraces, but he was so young. His eager chatter bored her, his incomprehension of matters that interested her was irritating. Ten years ago she would have been thrilled to have a football hero explain every play of a great game. Now—no. It was hard to hide her insulting indifference to his prowess on the football field.

And he cared nothing for music, art, theater, ballet. Ballet. She winced as she remembered his response when she suggested going. "That silly crap?" he had said. "See someone prancing around in tight pants? I should say not!"

He was very young. But a senior in college, she reminded herself. If he wasn't even faintly interested in the arts now, when would he develop interest? If he married a culturally alert girl, and she dragged him to concerts and museums, he might learn some day. More likely it was too late to instill any such interests in him.

Too bad. He was a nice boy—and very good in bed. But being good in bed wasn't enough to hold the attention of a woman like Claire who had high regard for mental as well as physical limberness.

After Claire's conversation with Wayne Kincaid and his brazen proposition to spend the holidays together, she made up her mind to go alone to New York to remove herself from all the crazy men in her life. She could use some new scenery and fresh ideas, she thought, packing her suitcases. There was some heavy thinking she ought to do, also, on the topic, namely, "How to keep Claire from becoming promiscuous." Last winter in Italy seemed to have demoralized her completely.

She decided to wait till she got to New York to buy play tickets. It was usually possible to pick up a single at the box office of any play except the current smash hits.

The last few days before the holidays were sufficiently hectic to justify putting Jerry off. "I'm too tired, much too exhausted, darling," she told him.

He was disappointed that she was going to New York. "I had sort of planned to stay on campus."

"Of course you shouldn't. Your family would be terribly disappointed." And his family might be smart enough to guess why he stayed, thought Claire in dismay.

"Couldn't we—just one night—before you go?" he begged.

She finally gave in and let him stay one night. He seemed especially tender, and insatiable as well. They went to bed early, soon after eight o'clock. She had hoped he would have enough to leave by midnight, so she could get some sleep.

She let him undress her as he liked to do, and then she lay back on the wide bed while he undressed. She gazed speculatively at his lean strong body, the long legs. What strange force was there, she thought, that made a man desire a woman? And that made a reluctant woman desire the embrace of a man she liked but did not love?

He came to the bed, stepping lightly on bare feet, and he crouched over her lovingly, his face lighting with passion. He bent over her and caressed her full breasts. He knew so well how to tease them until the nipples rose up full and pointed and then how to put the nipples in his mouth and tug at them until her whole body was aching for his caresses.

His hands explored her more closely. She clutched at his back. Her hips moved in eager rhythm to the impulses inside her.

Jerry smiled and began the movements to bring them together. Claire lay back in his embrace, her eyes closed, savoring the delicious excitement as his powerful thighs churned up desire. She enjoyed this, how she enjoyed it. If—if only ... What was wrong with her? Why did an if always enter her mind to steal some of her pleasure?

Jerry's long body slickened with sweat as he worked. She gripped harder, she wiggled enticingly under him. They moved in perfect rhythm to build up to a peak. Faster—faster—

Her mind blurred before the frantic sensations that stirred her blood. With closed eyes she swung up at the hips that were promising pleasure. She begged. "Jerry, do it, hard—"

He laughed aloud, a short excited bark. She felt sweet pain, sweet terrible pain—then a click through her whole body. Convulsions swept her, she could no longer control her limbs, she lay helpless while the sweetness overwhelmed her.

She felt Jerry's reactions to her, his own convulsions, the jerky rhythm as he fell helpless across her. They clung with lax hands as they finished.

He wanted her again soon. They had not been together for more than a week. His youthful body seemed to have stored up virile energy to explode in her time and again that night. She tired long before he did, and she lay weakly submissive to his eager masculine energy.

She wanted to sleep, but no sooner had she dozed off than she was awakened by lips on her throat, hands on her waist and thighs. Once she was deeply asleep and awakened with a jolt as Jerry entered her defenseless body. Her consciousness found him in full possession, and he was laughing softly as she looked up at him.

He finally left her about eight o'clock. Lucky it was Saturday morning. Claire moaned as she crawled out of bed. She tried to get dressed, but she was exhausted. She went back to bed and slept until late afternoon.

After that session, she knew she had to get away for a while. She couldn't take much more of this.

As soon as school broke for the holidays she returned to the apartment for her suitcases and called a taxi. She was on the train to New York within an hour.

She slept little that night although the Pullman berth was comfortable and the clack-clack of the train was monotonously soothing. How could she break off finally and completely with Jerry? How could she avoid him after the holidays when he was so confident that he could visit her apartment any time he pleased? Jerry was developing into a major problem. It didn't make the situation any easier that Claire herself was so weak where Jerry was concerned, her body impatient for the satisfaction he knew so well how to bestow.

It was her own fault, hers entirely, she admitted, peering at the nocturnal countryside rolling past. Dark trees, dark houses and a glimpse of a dark river intrigued her. All those people, and she passed by them in an instant, never knowing them, never thinking of them again—the people in the shacks near the railroad stations, the people in the house on the hill which had a window lit at three in the morning.

She lay back in the berth, staring at the walls of the room-ette, hoping sleep would come. She wanted to be fresh tomorrow when she arrived, to check into the hotel, have a bath, eat break-fast, then start out for the stores, the museums, the box offices for theater tickets. Where first?

Toward morning she fell into a light doze, and wakened with a jerk as the train pulled into Philadelphia. She decided to dress.

The train pulled into New York about ten o'clock. A porter deposited her and her luggage in a taxi, and soon she was regis-tering at the hotel Professor Lawson had recommended. It had been only a few months since she had been in New York, pausing there briefly on her way home from Italy. But it had been August, hot and sticky, and she had stayed only a day before going back to Dexter College.

Now she felt like a long leisurely vacation. She would sleep late, eat breakfast at noon, wander around, see all the plays and foreign movies she longed to see, enjoy being by herself and doing precisely what she pleased.

After Claire had checked in at the hotel, unpacked her suit-cases and had her bath, she went downstairs to the coffee shop for coffee and rolls. She bought a *New York Times,* a *New Yorker,* and the latest *Cue,* and she scanned the magazines as she ate. Up in her room she spread out the *Times* and studied the theater section absorbedly. She wrote down several plays she wanted to see.

She had kicked off her shoes, and sprawled across the bed to read the paper. Her eyes were heavy. She was groggy from sleep-lessness. She pushed the paper off the bed, and curled up. She would close her eyes for a few minutes. Then she would go and get some tickets and—

That was the last she remembered thinking. She woke up hours later, stiff, chilly. She hadn't even pulled up a blanket. She sat up with a great effort, glanced at her watch in the flickering lights of the neon sign outside her window. Six-thirty.

"Oh, no. All that time wasted," she muttered.

It was dark outside. The evening traffic roared by under the windows. The lights of Broadway glittered —the white lights, the red and blue and green neon lights. She stood at the window for several minutes, absorbed in the spectacle. Broadway—tarnished, frivolous, gawdy, spectacular, grand, beckoning.

Claire finally revived sufficiently to wash her face, renew her makeup and change her dress to a green velvet suit. She found a restaurant that served East Indian food, rice, lamb, chutney sauce, honey cake. Fortified, she headed for a theater and was able to obtain a single ticket for a play she wanted. For the next several hours she was totally absorbed in someone else's problems.

Afterwards she thought about having coffee somewhere, but she was too tired to stay out. She returned to the hotel, to bed and to sleep.

The next morning, she felt strong and clear-headed again. She decided to go to the Metropolitan Museum and see the paintings and the American wing. She had breakfast and started out.

It was mid-afternoon when she returned, having stopped at two bookstores to order books sent home. She walked briskly into the lobby, feeling pleasantly alone, completely unknown, unnoticed.

"Hello, Claire!" said a familiar deep voice.

She stared, aghast, stunned.

"Well, hello!" Wayne said again, laughing. "Imagine seeing you here."

He had followed her, she knew. Oh, the devil. How had he discovered where she was staying?

"Hello," she said curtly. "What are you doing in New York?"

"Your idea sounded good," he said brazenly. "I decided to take in some plays also. Haven't been to New York for years. How about going out with me tonight? We could see a play—"

"Im busy tonight," she said angrily, and brushed past him to stalk to the elevators. She was furious. Of all the gall, to follow her to New York. And how had he known where she was staying?

The next day Wayne insisted on having breakfast with her and chatting about the play he had seen the evening before. She was reluctantly interested in his comments and criticism.

"How about going out together today?" he said. "Where are you going?"

"That isn't your concern—I prefer to be by myself."

He only laughed, refusing to be insulted. She set out by herself after breakfast, and glanced back over her shoulder uneasily several times. She wasn't sure whether she dreaded seeing him or wanted to see him. It would have been nice to be able to discuss the paintings and sculpture at the Museum of Modern Art with someone who enjoyed art as much as he did.

When she arrived back at the hotel in mid-afternoon, there was a note in her mailbox from Wayne.

"I have two tickets for a play tonight. Meet you at six in the lobby. How about dinner at an Italian restaurant? Wayne."

He wasn't giving her a chance to turn him down. She was angry again. Of all the cocksure, impudent—She didn't intend to go with him. She would not go.

But she found herself choosing the dress she would wear, a vivid aqua silk with a boat neck, and her favorite dangling gold earrings.

After all, he might as well pay for her dinner and the play. If he were going to make himself obnoxious, he might as well be useful. She couldn't keep avoiding him.

He was waiting in the lobby at six. He seemed so sure and confident that she was very nearly tempted to breeze right past him and to turn up her nose at him as she made her exit.

But his face lit up on seeing her. "Claire, you're beautiful," he said.

Why were women such suckers for flattery? She was reluctantly pleased.

"I shouldn't go out with you. I'm very angry that you followed me to New York," she said bluntly.

"How could I help it? You are a strong irresistible magnet that allures me. I am helplessly, hopelessly, under your spell."

"Goon," she said.

He took her arm, grinned down at her. "Let's go, sweet. Italian restaurant okay?"

"Fine," she said with resignation. What was the use of fighting? He seemed to know just what he wanted, and went right after it.

It was fun to go out with Wayne, Claire found. He had a natural gaiety that was very appealing. He wasn't cynical all the time. Cynicism was a manner he seemed to adopt when it pleased him to do so.

He enjoyed life. He had many enthusiasms. It was good, Claire felt, to be with someone like Wayne who appreciated good paintings and sculpture, who knew and liked classic and modern music, who could browse for hours in a bookstore, who even enjoyed shopping for clothes with her.

Claire was rather suspicious when Wayne first suggested shopping with her. She thought he might be wanting to accompany her to laugh at styles or at her, or at both. She was pleasantly surprised at the keen interest he took in colors, lines, fashions.

She tried on a short black crepe dress he did not like. "I don't like black on you," he objected. "Deadens you. I hate black anyway."

"Black is always in style," said the grey-haired clerk, her hand moving defensively on her black threequartered sleeve.

Wayne looked deliberately at Claire's legs. More was revealed of them than usual in the short tight skirt. "Your knees are nice. Go ahead and get it, and give the boys a thrill."

She decided against that dress. He approved of the greens and blue-greens in style, but not a pastel blue.

"That's not for you. Too sticky sweet," he said.

She was tempted by a hat, very much in style, for spring. It was shaped like a funnel, and was covered with dozens of artificial flowers.

"Everyone is wearing a floral hat this spring, madame," the clerk said enthusiastically.

Claire tried it on. Some of the flowers dropped to her shoulders.

"Do you like it?" she asked Wayne, who was watching expressionlessly.

"Adore it," he said. "When you're tired of it, you can plant the flowers in a window box."

The clerk was outraged. Claire finally bought a sleek green velour pillbox and a beige brimmed straw for spring.

She wore the pillbox with her green silk dress to a play that evening. Wayne held her hand, and she felt eighteen and giddy.

It was fun to be with him in New York. He made an indecent suggestion every night before they parted, and she firmly refused each one. That was as far as he went in trying to have an affair with her. She was relieved—and slightly disappointed.

Christmas was soon there. They admired the tree at Rockefeller Center, heard Christmas music at several concerts, braved the crowds of shoppers. In one store Claire stopped still to stare.

Two of the most beautiful children she had ever seen stood beside a counter. They stood alone, backs, to the shelves, facing the crowds with calm patience. They seemed to belong to no one. The girl was about five, blond, wearing a ruby velvet coat and matching bonnet. She held the hand of a small boy of about two, blond also, with wide blue eyes and a trusting upturned face.

"Do you suppose they are lost?" Claire asked Wayne in concern.

"I don't think so. Their mother is probably nearby. Why do you worry so much about everybody else?"

It wasn't worry so much as envy, Claire thought, staring once more at the beautiful children until they were out of eyeshot. Those two lovely innocent faces haunted her the rest of the day. Children—to have children such as those. It gave her a frightened feeling to realize she was getting older and might never have children.

In spite of his apparent unconcern, Wayne had noticed and remembered the children also, because he spoke of them that evening.

"Those kids were so beautiful," he said. "I wonder if their parents appreciate them."

She gave him a quick glance. "Oh, I don't know. They were dressed well. But that might mean material care or pride, not genuine feeling for the children."

He said no more, but she was touched to learn of his interest. He wasn't hard and cynical as she had thought at first. Did he too want to marry, have children, take on the responsibilities and privileges of caring for a family?

She wasn't getting serious about him, was she? Looking back, she realized that in the past few days he had guided her touring, her choice of book purchases, her choice of clothes. She frowned, staring bemused at the lighted stage before them, but not hearing the words for a while. He was dominating her. She didn't want to be dominated. She was a free agent; she meant to stay that way.

Maybe it was only chance. She had chosen—he had approved her choices. Or had she bought items she would not have chosen otherwise? That green sweater. She hadn't intended to buy that, but he had admired it so extravagantly she had bought it. And she had been close to buying that black dress he had disliked. Black was always good for occasions, even though it wasn't her best color. Darn.

She made a conscious effort to resist his advice and control. It took more willpower, but she managed it. The day after Christmas she went out early in the morning and was alone. She told herself it was a relief to be alone.

There was a note for her in the mailbox when she returned to the hotel about three o'clock. "I have tickets for tonight—see you at six in the lobby—Wayne."

She wondered if he would be angry that she had walked out on him today. He showed no signs of anger at dinner, and talked cheerfully of his discoveries at the Museum of Natural History.

"What did you do today?" he wanted to know, over the glass of sparkling white wine.

"I went to the Frick," she said. "I like it there. I sat and looked at things."

"I like to do that. Sit still and let it sink in. I get tired of rushing, rushing all the time. Life is too short to let it go by so fast."

"Yes. Very short." She drank the rest of the wine in her glass, thinking again about the two children they had seen.

The play was amusing and quite suggestive. The husband was carrying on an affair with his wife's best friend. The wife finds out and in revenge begins an affair with the best friend's husband. The latter husband, surprised at his unexpected "conquest," cannot refrain from boasting to a mutual friend. The dialogue was brisk and full of innuendoes, and the second act took place in a bedroom.

Claire was accustomed to sophisticated plays, but she could feel her cheeks grow warm in the darkness as the situation developed on stage. The wine was heating her also. It didn't help when Wayne put his arm around her as a rather significant scene built up.

She whispered, "Don't do that," and she tried to push his arm away.

He paid no attention, seemingly completely absorbed in the play.

"Let go," she said more loudly.

The man behind her leaned forward. "Lady, I came to hear the play on the stage, not you."

Wayne chuckled. Claire could have disappeared through the floor, she was so embarrassed.

At the end of act two, the curtains closed on two of the main characters climbing into bed.

"Aw, shucks," said Wayne in Claire's ear. "I'd like to see the next ten minutes."

The lights came on.

"Did you get tickets for this play on purpose?" she demanded. She could have bet her face was as red as the curtains on the stage.

He looked mildly surprised. "Don't you like it? It had some good reviews."

The third act was a letdown as the play worked toward its conventional happy ending and husbands and wives were sorted out and put back in their places again.

"Let's go to Lindy's for cheesecake," Wayne suggested.

Claire was feeling cross and perverse. "I'm tired. I'm going back to the hotel."

"Okay," he agreed amiably.

At the hotel, he saw her to her room but then, instead of leaving, he walked in the door after her and closed it.

"I could use a little more wine. How about you?" Before she could say no, he had lifted the telephone receiver and was dialing room service. He ordered champagne.

She was thirsty, and it was rather early. And he hadn't tried to rape her this week. She kicked off her high-heeled shoes, put on bedroom slippers, and relaxed in the arm chair. Wayne cleared off a corner of her desk by shoving papers and books aside.

The bellboy brought the champagne and glasses. The ice bucket was full of ice, the wine chilled to perfection. The boy opened the bottle, and it gave a satisfactory pop.

"I'll pour it. Thanks very much." Wayne shooed him out, closed and locked the door.

Claire decided she had no reputation left. The next time she came to New York she would choose a new hotel without making reservations in advance. She still would give a lot to know how Wayne had found out.

Wayne filled their glasses, handed Claire hers. He clicked the glasses, rim to rim. "To us," he said solemnly. "And lots of fun in the New Year."

"It isn't New Year yet."

"It will be in a few days."

They sipped their wine. The champagne drove straight to her head and made her feel light and bubbly and pleasantly irresponsible. She didn't mean to get drunk tonight.

Wayne discussed the play. "That third act was flat. So often that happens. Why does the third act flatten out? As far as I was concerned it could have ended with the second-act curtain."

"No. The moral would be lost. And plays nowadays have to end with a moral, even though there isn't any other moral in the whole play."

"You're right. You are absolutely right." He refilled their glasses. "To plays without morals."

They drank to that. She wasn't sure why. They also drank to the actors who had gotten into bed. "Poor kids. They had to get right out again and change their clothes for the next act. No time for fun," said Wayne.

"Too bad." Claire giggled. "Wouldn't it be funny if some night they got carried away and forgot it was a play?"

They laughed. It sounded like a great idea. "Method acting carried to its logical conclusion," Wayne said.

They discussed writing a play together. They had several great ideas for plays.

"How about a play about a man who falls in love with a woman and marries her and beats her up until she falls in love with him?"

Claire frowned. "That's old. That's in *The Taming of the Shrew*. Willie did that one."

"Old Willie. Good ol' Willie Shakespeare. Long may he write plays. To Willie."

They drank the next one to Willie.

Claire began to feel giddy. She managed to stand up and set her glass beside the ice bucket. "No more for me—I feel funny."

"Are you sleepy?" asked Wayne.

"I sure am. You go on home. I've got to get some sleep." She managed to walk over to the bed and fell across it.

Wayne set down his glass, and took off her slippers. "You're tired. You're sleepy," he said. "I'll help you go to bed."

"I don't need help." But her bones felt funny, all fluid and lax. She did not resist as he unzipped her dress and started to pull it off. He helped her sit up, and slid the dress over her head. He pulled up the slip, drew it off. Then he unfastened the brassiere, took that off.

"I'm cold," said Claire.

"I'll warm you," he said. He opened the covers, rolled her inside the sheets, then pulled off her panties and stockings. He covered her again, and she closed her eyes and yawned.

"Good night," she said sleepily.

He did not answer. Pretty soon, very soon, he got in bed beside her. He was naked also. Claire felt vaguely disturbed. She ought to protest, but it did no good to protest to Wayne. He went ahead and did whatever he wanted.

His body was warm and hard against hers, warming her. His arm was hard under her neck. His hand was hard and big, squeezing her breast. She moved uneasily, trying to pull away. Her body was getting warm, too warm.

His mouth touched hers, opened, forced hers to open. His tongue touched her tongue, and it tasted of wine, she thought dizzily. She tasted his lips with her tongue, and his lips were sweet as wine. Their open mouths pressed together. His tongue explored her mouth, her teeth, her tongue, the sensitive flesh of the roof of her mouth. She slipped her tongue inside his mouth because of the wine taste.

His hand stroked her big soft breasts, teasing the nipples, teased them till they rose taut and hard. He was rough with her breasts, rubbing them, crushing them. She muttered a protest.

His big hand went to her waist, sliding over her, caressed her, moved on roughly to her hips and thighs; he rubbed her knee, then rubbed above the knee inside her thighs. His hand rose higher between her thighs.

Heat was sweeping through her body. She was so sleepy. If he would only caress her gently, she could go to sleep. He was keeping her awake. Her knees jerked spasmodically. She tried to roll over in bed, to escape him. Impossible.

If only she wasn't so sleepy. If only her hips were stronger and could throw him off. She did try to evade him. She wiggled her hips desperately with what energy she could command, trying to dodge his turning thrusting loins. But he bent closer, searched, found, held her steady and jolted into her triumphantly.

Waves of sweetest ecstasy shot through her. Her hands slipped on his chest and went around him to clutch at his back. She hugged him to her fiercely to increase the pleasure. The peak was completed too soon.

But he stayed with her and played with her body in his ruthless way. He slid back and forth, his hands rough, his breath panting at her breasts. And the sweetness came again for her. This time he, too, experienced the high pleasure—convulsive movements wrenched his body until he lay sprawled across her.

They slept later. She wakened some time in the night to find him asleep with his arms around her. The champagne had worn off. Her brain was clear once more. But this time she was not angry.

She was in his arms, waiting, her mouth soft and ready, her body soft for his hardness. He kissed her till their bodies could not wait to meet, and they rushed together with frantic impatience. Under him she waited with closed eyes and yielded to his attack.

They embraced again, falling asleep in the middle. They wakened, continued, finding new avenues of pleasure. They learned each other's arms and legs and hips and torsos. She shivered in rapture too fierce to be endured, and tried to pull away from his experimental caressing.

"Don't—not like—that—don't—"

"Let me. Let me do everything."

He had his way, and she submitted completely to his domination. He forced her to admit her joy.

"You liked it. Didn't you?" he said.

"No—no—"

"Tell me. I'll do it again—"

"Oh, Wayne, you do too much. Don't—not so hard—"

"I want you. Tell me you liked it. You shivered. I could feel you shivering."

"Wayne—"

"Tell me—" His husky voice in her ears, his hands on her body, his hips rubbing against hers—were too much.

"I did. I did like it," she said.

"You want it again."

"No," she said.

"Yes."

"Yes. Yes. Yes."

He caressed her with lips and tongue, with hands and body, with relentless, terrifying, thorough osculations and touches that obliterated all else for her in the world. There was no reality but his voice in the darkness, his demands, his tongue on her sensitive flesh, his kisses in unexpected places, the piercing of her flesh.

In the morning when it was light, she tried to deny him. But he laughed at her, softly, and took her again. He stayed till late afternoon, insatiable, rough when she resisted, sweet when she yielded completely.

Her own flesh had betrayed her. He was ruthless in taking advantage of her weakness. They lived together the remainder of the holidays. They went everywhere together, walking, talking, seeing, listening. And always they went back early to her room, and fell across the bed in an ecstasy of desire.

She could not deny him. He had crowded in, bullied his way into possession, and she could not push him away. She didn't even want to resist him—for a while.

They celebrated New Year's Eve with more champagne in her bedroom. This time the ice bucket was beside the bed, and they were in bed. And the toasts were different. Wayne toasted Claire from head to foot—and everywhere in between.

It was a very satisfactory way to begin a new year.

CHAPTER SEVEN

ELSIE ZECK had been acquiring a liberal sex education during the past three months. Her teachers had been several of the most expert men on campus. She had learned the art of kissing in both its normal and exotic forms, the techniques of necking, the skills of petting and, of course, the craft of intercourse.

The only thing she had not learned was how to attract Jerry Arnold's attention. He was supremely indifferent to her. She had seen him on and off campus. He was usually alone and seemed content to be so. There was a rumor that he was seeing a lot of one of the teachers, Miss Frazier, but Elsie wasn't sure how true the rumor was.

Elsie had been very busy socially and much in demand. She knew why. The boys considered her an easy mark now. That was the price she paid for her education. It was nice to have the phone ringing constantly for her, to be asked to all the dances, parties, events. But she knew what they wanted and expected from her.

Secretly she wondered if all girls attained their popularity at this cost. She would look at some of the girls on campus, and wonder. Did they or didn't they? How far did they go?

She had several regular fellows now. Each was jealous of the other, but she shrugged off their demands to be a "steady." She didn't want to go steady with any of them. They were all a means to one end—Jerry. She wanted Jerry—that was why she had acquired her sex education, to attract and hold Jerry. He was older, sophisticated, smart. No naive innocent for him, she felt. Well, now she was ready for him.

But he didn't notice her at all. She saw him often in class, on campus, in the college hangouts, but he smiled, said "Hi, there," and walked on.

Dan Evans asked Elsie to the frat dance in January. She had bought a new formal at Christmas time when she was home. It was a strapless red net with a frilly short skirt that showed her dimpled knees. Her mother had protested weakly.

"All the girls wear them, Mother," Elsie had said firmly, and she had bought it.

Dan was crazy about the package. He kept staring at her as they danced. Once in a dim corner he put his head down and kissed her shoulder near the throat. It sent a thrill down her spine.

But Jerry Arnold didn't see Elsie for dust. He had come stag and was dancing only once with each girl. Elsie waited impatiently for Jerry to approach her.

It was only after intermission that he got around to her. With a sigh of relief, Elsie moved into his arms. He held her loosely, as though scarcely aware of her as a person.

She would change all that, she vowed. She crowded in, put up her hand high on his shoulder. Then her fingers touched his neck.

"You've been avoiding me," she accused.

"Avoiding? No, I haven't."

"Yes, you have. Ever since that time on campus last fall. When I got soaked and all the fellows stared."

He smiled, looked at her as though he finally saw her. She felt his gaze on her creamy white shoulders. He studied the swell of her breasts revealed by the top of the red net dress.

"If they hadn't stared, I would have figured they weren't normal," he said.

"You haven't been staring," she accused softly, smiling up at him, her eyes narrowed tantalizingly.

His arm tightened. She felt a swift thrill of hope. The dance ended.

He stepped away from her. Dan was standing right there.

"Thanks for the dance, Elsie," said Jerry pleasantly, and walked away to pause before another girl.

Elsie wanted to stamp her foot and throw a tantrum. She was so disappointed she wanted to scream. She had been so sure he would ask her for another dance, give her a chance to attract him, encourage him to ask for a date.

Dan took her in his arms for the next dance. "Elsie, sweet, you're gorgeous. Let's go out in the car for a while," he muttered in her ear. Then he kissed her ear slowly.

She was in no mood for back-seat romancing. It was awkward and she got cold, too. January weather was no fun in a convertible.

She was angry at Jerry for brushing her off. He still wasn't convinced she was a mature woman. She had an idea. Once the word of this episode got around, Jerry would be convinced.

"Dan," she whispered. "I'm tired of cars. Why don't we go to a motel where we can relax and have a real good time?"

Dan's eyes widened. He flushed. "You mean it? For sure?"

'Sure," she said recklessly. "Let's go now."

He was ready. She paused to murmur to her roommate, "Harriet, sign me in when you get back. And don't worry —I won't be returning until morning."

"Elsie," Harriet groaned, "don't be crazy. Wait—tell me?"

But Elsie grinned impudently, waved her hand and found her wrap.

Dan knew a motel about twenty miles away where no one asked awkward questions about luggage or age. Elsie waited in the car while Dan registered them. He came back with a key.

"Number twenty-four," he said briefly, and drove the car up to the door of that cabin.

Elsie hopped out of the car, the wind hitting her knees and making her shiver. She felt hot and angry and eager all at once.

She would show Jerry. After this night with Dan, Jerry wouldn't think she was young and naive. She was every bit as good at sex as that Miss Frazier, whom they said he was crazy about.

Dan locked the door after them. Elsie took off her wrap and tossed it on a chair. Dan took her in his arms and started kissing her all over her neck and shoulders.

"Wait," said Elsie, pushing him away.

Dan started to get angry. "You're not going to get me here, and then say no, are you?" he demanded.

She laughed tantalizingly. "Have I said no to you yet? You sit down on the bed and watch me."

He sat down on the edge of the bed. She tried to reach the zipper at the back of her dress but couldn't. She backed up to him. "Unzip me."

She felt his cold hands clumsily on the zipper, felt him lower it to below her waist. She let the dress fall down to her waist, stepped away from him, turned to face him again.

She drew the dress down over her hips, stepped out of it daintily and hung it over the chair. She kicked off her red slippers. She unfastened her hose, bent, rolled the stockings off, threw them on the chair. She drew off the filmy red slip and stood revealed in a red strapless bra and a thin girdle.

She stretched and turned before him. He was staring at her, his eyes glazed. He started to get off the bed.

"Wait," she said. Slowly, provocatively, she unfastened the bra, let it slide off her full breasts.

Dan gasped, reached for her yearningly.

"Wait," she whispered. He watched like a man in a happy trance.

The girdle was rolled off her hips, down over her thighs, below her knees. She stepped out of her girdle and pitched it on to the chair and came over to the bed. She stood naked before him, pressing herself against his shaking knees.

"Now you," she said, and began to unfasten his tie. She took it off, helped him off with his coat, unfastened his shirt.

She laughed with delight as he reacted strongly. He pushed her down on the bed and he flung off the rest of his clothes in a frenzy.

In a few moments he had joined her on the bed. Their hot young bodies flowed together like molten lava. He wrestled her over on her back and she writhed until he held her down strongly with his muscular thighs. She forgot everything but the sheer physical delight of their pleasure. Sparks were set off inside her; he ignited her body like dry tinder.

He had his satisfaction too soon, and he rolled away from her. She was impatient to continue to find her own release. She leaned over him, teased his body with skillful fingers.

"Honey, you're driving me out of my mind," he groaned, his body arching.

She giggled. "That's how I want you—out of your mind."

He was soon ready for another attack. This time she was the aggressor. His strong thighs lurched under her.

"Don't buck so," she cried, laughing.

"You're a living doll," he said, laughing too. She crouched over him, bouncing, feeling the weakness stealing over her as she moved.

His hard hands pulled her closer, held her. Then she lay across his body, drowning in ecstasy as she hit the acme of bliss.

They collapsed together, side by side, still tangled, wet with perspiration, their hands sliding from each other's bodies.

She stayed with him all night. Neither slept. They played roughly, eager to riot in the other's nakedness, eager to match desire for desire, eager to snatch pleasure with greedy hands.

Late the next morning he took her back to the dorm. She crept in the side door and up to her room. Harriet was at class.

Elsie stripped, took a shower and went to bed. Jerry ought to find out soon from the gossip what kind of girl she was.

Her strip tease in front of Dan had given her another idea.

Dan called her that evening and wanted to go out again soon. She told him she wanted to go to the basketball rally on Wednesday night.

"The rally? Elsie, what do you want with that kid stuff? I want more of last night."

She laughed softly, teasingly. "Oh, did you enjoy that?"

"You're the greatest, you're the sweetest—"

She listened to his vivid exotic description of her charms with pleased attention. But her mind was concentrated on another man.

"The rally, then, Wednesday," she said firmly.

"But what about us?" he wailed.

She could control him. "Maybe later in the week, Dan. I'm tired—you did an awful lot to me last night."

He laughed, satisfied, and promised to take her to the rally.

On Wednesday night they sat in the middle of the crowd of students on the bleachers in the gym. The basketball team had won its first game and, as everyone loves a victorious team, a big crowd had turned out to cheer the players on. Elsie kept on her black coat and waited tensely through the speeches by the college president, the athletic director, and the coaches.

Finally they began bringing out the players, one by one, starting with the least valuable players. Elsie watched, cold fists in her coat pockets, her cheeks burning hot.

At last they reached the top players. The crowd applauded more violently, cheers rocking the gym. Students were jumping up and down, yelling, clapping.

The coach screamed into the mike. "And now—captain of the team—most valuable player—senior Jerry Arnold—"

Elsie stood up and took off her black coat. Behind her several students yelped, "Down in font—sit down—down down in front there.

She paid no attention. Jerry had run out on the floor, big and handsome in his white shirt and white shorts. He grinned up at the crowd, waved, clasped his hands above his head.

The students were led in a cheer. Elsie flung her coat down on the bench beside Dan. He grasped her arm, tried to pull her down beside him. She jerked away.

She was wearing a brilliant red cardigan sweater and a black skirt. Deliberately she unfastened the buttons of the sweater and took it off, flinging it in Dan's face as he tried to stop her.

Some students in front turned to stare at her. She watched Jerry as she unfastened the zipper at the side of the skirt. He was looking up toward her. He was seeing her, at last.

She stripped off the black skirt.

"For the love of Mike—Elsie—cut that out—" Dan tried to yank her down beside him. Elsie, in her thin red slip, pulled away.

A campus guard was starting up the steps toward her. Several teachers in a row nearby jumped up, white faces turned toward her. She wanted to laugh at them. Silly people. Because Jerry was looking at her, Jerry was staring at her.

She took the hem of the slip in her hands, pulled it upward, pulled off the slip. She stood proudly, clad only in a red brassiere and a thin pair of red panties.

Now she heard the screaming. Men, yelling, "Take it off-take it off—that's the stuff—take it off—"

A teacher reached her. Miss Frazier. Hateful Miss Frazier. Elsie jerked away from her, tried to reach the fastenings of the brassiere to take it off. The taller woman reached for her again, shook her violently.

"Elsie, stop this," Miss Frazier commanded.

Elsie tried again to get at the fastenings of the brassiere. Jerry was looking. She wanted him to see her breasts, really see them—

"Put her coat around her," Miss Frazier ordered.

Dan, behind Elsie, flung the heavy winter coat around her, trapping her arms. Miss Frazier fastened the buttons. Elsie couldn't get loose. She screamed, angrily. "Let me alone, let me go—you have no right—"

The guard had reached them. Dan, Miss Frazier and the guard carried Elsie down the steps of the bleachers and out the side door of the gym. Elsie was crying with rage and frustration. If only they had let her finish—if only Jerry had seen how beautiful and desirable her body was—

They took her to the clinic. Miss Frazier sent Dan away, and she and the nurse talked to Elsie sternly until the doctor arrived.

Miss Frazier was very angry and concerned. "That was a dreadful tiling to do. How could you do that? What possessed you? In front of that crowd—you ought to be spanked!"

"You could have caused a riot," said the nurse fussily. "You're a bad girl. What kind of a reputation—"

"Why did you do it? Why?" asked hateful Miss Frazier, who had taken Jerry away from her.

Elsie wept with frustration. "I don't know why I did it," she sobbed, because they expected her to say these words. "I don't know why I did it."

If only she had been allowed to finish.

Claire Frazier was very concerned about Elsie Zeck. The girl seemed to have changed character completely since September. Claire wondered if the girl were insane.

She spoke to Wayne about Elsie. She and Wayne had had a couple dates since the holidays, but only innocent dates involving dinner and concerts. Claire was wary of any more bedroom sessions with Wayne until she had her own feelings sorted out.

"The girl wanted to attract attention," said Wayne. "And she sure attracted mine. What a figure," he finished gustily.

"Men," sighed Claire. "But why did she do that strip at just that moment?"

"Rumor has it she's been chasing that basketball hero—what's his name? Jerry something. Jerry Arnold."

"Oh," said Claire. Now she felt guilty. She couldn't look Wayne in the face. What a mess. If only she could break off with Jerry. She had tried. She had thought their absence from each other during the holidays would help cut off their relations.

Quite the contrary had occurred. Jerry came back more eager than ever, more confident.

Claire wondered if he were neglecting basketball practice, or his studies. He seemed to have too much time on his hands. She protested to Jerry when he came over on Sunday morning.

"Jerry, you can't keep on like this. All the basketball games, and your classes—"

"Don't worry about me. I'm strong." He swept her off her feet to prove it, dumped her on the couch, and followed her down, to kiss her greedily. She tried to push his head away from her face so she could speak.

"Jerry, let me talk. I'm concerned. You're spending too much time up here—"

His eager young body was pressing closer. He pulled up her skirt, opened her clothes, and in a moment he had joined their bodies. Her protests died away...

If only she weren't so weak about this, she thought later as she let him sleep on her breast. She caressed his blond head with light fingers. He could be so sweet, so lovable. And his strong young body was becoming more skillful all the time.

But how long could this go on? Could she count on his growing weary of her, breaking off the relationship in time? He would graduate in June. That would break it off. January, February, March, April, May. Five months. What if Wayne found out? What if Wayne knew already?

She wasn't sure how she felt about Wayne. He was too dominating. He made her do what he wanted. He made her speak truthfully about her feelings and emotions. He was ruthless in stripping off films of pretense. If she accepted him as her lover, or took him as a husband, she would have to give up her independence, her freedom to do as she pleased.

She wasn't sure she wanted to marry anyone as masculine as Wayne. Wouldn't it be better to find someone over whom she would have more control? Besides, Wayne didn't want marriage. He was as happy, single, as she was. He wasn't about to give up his freedom, either. So it followed that all he wanted from her was an affair. Wasn't that what she wanted also?

She stirred restlessly. Jerry wakened, and turned to her confidently, his hand on her breast. She let him caress her. He slipped his hand under the sweater, sought the top of the slip, pulled the slip strap down and uncovered a breast. He held the soft flesh in his palm, squeezing it

"Jerry, I've been thinking," she said.

"I'll soon stop that," he said, bending over and putting his mouth to the nipple of the breast he was fondling.

"I mean it, Jerry. We must not keep on and on like this. We have to stop."

"No." He went on.

She pushed him away a little so she could look into his eyes. "I mean it. We can't drift on and on."

"Yes, we can."

"Jerry, I'm years older than you. You're only twenty. I'm thirty."

"I'm twenty-one, almost twenty-two."

"You ought to be thinking about girls your own age." She thought of Elsie Zeck trying desperately to attract Jerry's attention. "You ought to be dating the college girls. What's wrong about this is it's preventing you from considering your own future."

"I'm happy." He opened the belt of her skirt, unfastened the side zipper, slid the skirt off her legs. He drew up the thin slip, caressed her bare knees and thighs with long strokes, his palm warm.

Presently she wouldn't have the strength to argue.

"Jerry, I want to break off. I don't want to go on. We have to stop."

"Are you tired of me?" he asked, the teasing gone from his voice. She couldn't see his face. He was kissing her waist.

"Oh, Jerry."

"Are you tired of me? Do you want me to stop bothering you? Is that it?"

If she told him yes, he would go, hurt, his ego bruised. She couldn't hurt him like that He was a wonderful lover. He had been good to her, good and exciting, filling a need in her for more lovemaking like Gino's.

"I'm not tired of you, Jerry. I love it, what you do to me. You know that" She caressed his head tenderly.

"Then why?"

"I'm too old for you. You ought to date younger girls. You ought to think of marriage."

His hand moved steadily on her, building up her passions. He said, confidently, "I don't want to think of anything like marriage. Younger girls bore me. I want you. You're what I want."

She was spoiling him for girls his own age. He was experimenting with her, making discoveries about a woman that should have waited for the girl he would marry. It troubled her, not for the first time, what she was doing to Jerry.

"Well have to break off, Jerry. We can't go on. We must break it off, even though we don't want to."

He shook his head. "No," he said, flatly. "No, I won't. There's nothing wrong with this. We're not hurting anybody. We both know what we are doing. I won't stop."

She went on protesting until his tongue searched her mouth, touched the roof, moved slowly inside her lips. Oh, he was sweet, sweet as honey, sweet as candied honey. She put her tongue inside his lips and tasted of his sweetness and his youth and his eagerness. Their arms tightened around each other, their bodies became impatient.

Then she said his name as his mouth kissed her cheeks, her throat. Her clothes were in the way. He made her sit up, and he stripped off her sweater and then her slip that had ridden up above her waist.

"Let's go in the bedroom," he said then. "I like to roll you across the bed."

His muscular loins ground at her. His body grew slippery under her hands. It was hot in the room, hot and dim, and they were alone. No one would know. And she wanted so much. What did it matter what they did? It didn't hurt anyone. It was their own business.

She gave herself to him in a mighty frenzy of passion, matching his thrusts with her counter-thrusts, sliding her hips under his, gripping at him with her long smooth legs. Then he held her down to finish, bursting into dark waves of fire and storm. She blacked out with the ecstatic bursts of her own response.

They were too weak at the last to let go of each other. They collapsed across the bed, still gripping each other, still entangled. She gasped, trying to get her breath. She heard him breathing as though after a race.

Then he said, "Am I still too young for you?"

"Oh—Jerry—Jerry—"

He laughed, brokenly, his arms still around her. And she knew that in his young exuberance he would soon take her again.

CHAPTER EIGHT

WOMEN were funny, decided Professor Wayne Kincaid. He had scarcely seen Claire after their passionate days and nights. They had returned to the college campus on separate trains. She had insisted on that.

Since school had begun again, he hadn't had a real date with her. He couldn't lure her within blocks of his apartment.

And he knew, he knew damn well, she had thoroughly enjoyed their sessions together. She might have been drunk that first time, but she sure hadn't been drunk all week. How she could love—he shivered with remembered delight. She was a wonderful, passionate, experienced woman, and he was crazy to have her again.

What was wrong with her, anyway? Why did she have these fits of prudery? He knew how to be cautious. He wasn't going to flaunt their affair in the faces of college authority. Why wouldn't she trust him on the campus as well as in New York?

It was exasperating and tantalizing to have dinner with her, to sit next to her at a concert, to hold her hand, touch her knee, want her with heavy desire—and then to have to take her home and be satisfied with a brief farewell kiss. What was her game? What was she up to? Why couldn't she let him come in her apartment for only a few hours at least?

Claire was quite firm about it. No more affair with Wayne, not on campus. And when he tried to insist on meeting her somewhere off campus for a weekend, she turned cold and refused all dates for the next several weeks. He could have shaken her till her teeth rattled.

About the middle of February he was asked to help chaperon a fraternity dance. He didn't care much about that sort of thing. Two married couples had also been asked. He figured that if the kids really wanted to commit adultery out in their cars, six chaperons wouldn't stop them, or sixty, either. It all seemed rather foolish, oldfashioned, and blandly optimistic.

However, the dance offered a good excuse to get Claire out on a date with him. She took her teaching duties very seriously.

It worked. She agreed to go. Wayne could have cursed when he saw how she was dressed. Instead of wearing one of the daring, gorgeous dresses she had worn in New York, she wore an overly demure dark green dinner dress with three-quarter sleeves, a high neckline, and a skirt to her ankles.

"What the hell possessed you to wear that sack?" he demanded, his esthetic senses outraged. "You look like your grandmother."

"I'm a chaperon, remember?" she said frigidly.

"That doesn't mean you can't have any fun at all," said Wayne, wistfully.

"Yes, it does," said Claire. She seemed bent on Doing Her Duty. She danced dutifully one dance with Wayne, one with each of the chaperon professors and one with the president of the fraternity. Then she sat at one of the ridiculous little tables, a glass of non-alcoholic punch at hand, and observed the dancers with the unconcealed anxiety of a mother hen. She paid no further attention to Wayne than absolutely necessary.

Wayne was about to ask her for another dance when one of the campus heroes came up, young Jerry Arnold.

"May I have this dance?" he said to Claire.

She got up and went with him. They danced three dances before he brought her back. When Jerry had left Claire at the table and stalked away, Wayne said sharply, "You must like young pups."

Claire's fair face flushed. She fiddled with the warm glass of punch. "What can I do? Refuse?" she said.

Wayne sulked. Then he saw another young man approaching. "I want this dance," Wayne snapped at Claire before the boy could come closer.

They danced, but her lithe body that could be so yielding and passionate in bed was stiff and inflexible. He tried to draw her closer, but she would draw away each time, even risking a stumble. He took her back to the table and wished the faculty allowed the students to have drinks at their dances. This faculty member needed a drink.

Jerry Arnold came back. "May I have this dance?" he said to Claire.

Wayne was surprised. The boy had done his duty by the chaperon. It was unusual to ask a second time.

Claire's fair face flushed bright red. "Why—ah—" She looked helplessly at Wayne.

"Go ahead," said Wayne, not liking the situation one bit.

They danced two dances before they returned. Claire was walking several paces ahead of Jerry. Wayne heard the end of an argument.

"No. Not again," she said.

"Just once more," said Jerry, huskily.

"No. I told you."

She sat down at the table. Jerry, after a lingering glance, departed.

"How about some refreshments?" Wayne suggested. They sauntered over to the buffet tables and filled plates with sandwiches and appetizers. Claire's face gradually cooled to its normal color from the hot pink it had been.

They sat down with another chaperoning couple who had trouble concealing yawns.

"I always say I'll never go to another dance. Then Jean talks me into it," the professor complained. "Why can't they get someone else?"

"Because all the girls are crazy about you, dear," said Jean, winking at Wayne. "They call me and beg us to come to their dances, just so they can dance with you."

"Piffle," said the professor.

"He enjoys it, too," Jean confided to Wayne, her grey head tipped to one side, observing her embarrassed husband with mischievous eyes. "Makes him feel young again, to hold these gay things in his arms."

Claire choked on a pickle. Wayne pounded her back efficiently.

One of the gay things came up to their table and said to Wayne, "Professor Kincaid, you haven't asked me to dance."

"Ha," said Jean softly.

Wayne allowed himself to be dragged away. She was a cute thing with big blue eyes and a dazzling smile, wearing very little on her innocently sensuous body. He enjoyed himself thoroughly, and began to change his low opinion of frat dances.

When he came back to the table for four, Claire had disappeared.

"One of the boys asked her to dance," said the prof.

"Jerry, his name is," said Jean.

"Jerry Arnold?"

"That's right."

Wayne sat down. A strong suspicion was growing. Jerry certainly had a crush on Claire, and it was becoming more and more obvious that Claire didn't know how to control the boy. He was surprised at Claire. She had been teaching for years. Surely she had handled this kind of problem before.

It was almost half an hour before Claire and Jerry returned. She didn't even speak to the boy when he held her chair for her.

"Nice dance, good music," said Jean kindly to Jerry, to cover an awkward hush.

"Yes, ma'am." He gave Claire a long slow look, then departed.

"He sure does have a yen for you," said Jean cheerfully to Claire. "Or is he bucking for a higher grade?"

"His grades are all right," said Claire shortly. She excused herself to go to the ladies room.

When Wayne took her home about two in the morning, he questioned her sharply about Jerry.

"Can't you control a boy with a crush? Everyone commented on it. That can make trouble."

"He's just a boy," Claire snapped peevishly.

"He's quite a boy. Six feet tall and a hero on campus. He scarcely danced with anyone but you." Wayne stopped the car outside her apartment and turned to her seriously. "You refuse to go out with me very often because of talk. Well, this kind of behavior can cause a lot more talk than the dating of two professors."

"It won't happen again," she promised. "I'll speak to him. Now, let me alone." She put her hand on the door handle.

"Wait a minute." Wayne forgot all about Jerry. He remembered only that he had been out for hours with this tantalizing woman, and hadn't kissed her once. He put his arms around her demandingly. Claire turned her head away sharply. But, he kissed her soft perfumed throat, kissed the ear and the twist of blond hair. "Claire," he whispered. "Claire."

She kept her head turned away. Her shoulders were stiff. He kissed her throat, the soft hollow where a pulse beat hard under his seeking lips.

"I want to come up," he whispered. "Claire, a few hours —" He hadn't meant to beg, but he wanted her desperately. "Claire, please, a few hours—"

"No." She pulled away, opened the car door. A blast of cold air chilled him. "Good night," she said curtly, and she slammed the door. He watched her run up to her apartment house door, open it, slam it behind her.

He started the car with a roar. What a waste of an evening this had turned out to be, he thought furiously. The next time he took Claire out he would get her good and drunk and bring her back to his place and keep her there for a long time. That seemed to be the only treatment that worked with her.

Undressing that night, he pondered Claire's strange behavior, and Jerry Arnold's strange confidence. He couldn't help feeling there was something going on between the two. Was it more than a crush on Jerry's part? Was there more than a student-teacher relationship?

Or was it only that Wayne believed Claire was stronger than she really was? She seemed strong, vital, sure of herself. Maybe she wasn't. Maybe she really could not handle a starry-eyed student who fell at her feet and worshipped. He didn't blame Jerry for falling—he had good taste enough to appreciate a gorgeous woman.

But Wayne didn't like Claire's reactions. A warning bell was ringing in his mind. As he dropped off to sleep, he thought he would have to find out more about Jerry.

Claire was furiously angry at Jerry for the scene he had caused at the frat dance. Wayne had been surprised and suspicious, and she couldn't blame him. Jerry had behaved outrageously.

This was the very behavior she had feared. She should have broken off with Jerry Arnold long ago, long before he got the cocky self-confidence to make an open play for her in front of everyone. She might have known she couldn't have hoped to keep the affair hidden indefinitely.

She fumed at herself and at Jerry until she could see him again. Finally he appeared on Wednesday evening.

"Come in," she said curtly. Their affair was probably being broadcast all over the campus. Did he have to be so noisy about it?

He was beaming, happy, childishly gay. Basketball practice had gone well, and they had been dismissed early. She listened to him sullenly, resenting his youth, his carefree nonchalance. It didn't matter to him what happened to her reputation.

Finally his exuberant chatter died away. "What's the matter, Claire?" he asked in concern. "Do you feel sick?"

"No. I'm not sick." She leaned back on the couch and watched him with detachment. How could she have been so crazy about such a boy? He wasn't much more than a child. "I'm angry at you, Jerry," she said.

"Angry? What did I do?" He really didn't know.

"That scene at the frat dance. What were you trying to do? Advertise our affair? Make it rough for me?"

He looked blank. His mouth fell open, he stammered in astonishment before he spoke.

"What? No, I wasn't trying to make it rough for you. Good gosh, Claire. I didn't mean to do anything. I just wanted to dance with you. I couldn't stand to see you with all the other fellows."

What would he say, she thought, if he ever learned of the New York episode with Wayne Kincaid? She shuddered to think of his jealousy. He could create quite an unpleasant scene.

She got up her courage. She must finish this. She couldn't risk any more exposure. She had been rash and foolish to begin this affair, to say nothing of allowing it to continue so long.

"This is the end, Jerry," she said. "We can't go on. It will make trouble."

He flung himself at her, clasping her knees in his arms. "No, Claire, no! I'll stay away from you in public, I promise. You won't have to worry any more about that"

"No, Jerry. I should have broken off long ago." "I won't let you stop. I love you. I'm crazy about you."

"I told you before, this can't go on and on." She looked away from his pleading face. "It had to stop some time, Jerry. I'm bad for you."

"No, you aren't. I need you. I go crazy when I'm away from you."

"All the more reason to break off." She forced her voice to remain cool and firm. "You're gotten used to me. You take me for granted. You have to leave in June anyway. We wouldn't see each other after that."

"We could spend the summer together, we could go away—"

"No. It's silly to think so."

"Then let's go on till June. Don't break off till June."

She hesitated. But if she gave in again and let the affair go on till June, the relationship would be all the more difficult to break off. Jerry was getting too accustomed to lovemaking, too used to having what he wanted from a woman.

And there was the risk now of being observed. Faculty and students had seen Claire and Jerry together at the dance. They were taking too big a chance to continue the affair. She was impatient with all the hiding and lying. She wanted to cut off, clear away, be honest again.

"No, Jerry," she said firmly. She shoved him away from her knees. "No more of this. We must stop now. The campus has started talking about us."

"And you care about that more than you care about me?" He leaned back on his heels, staring at her, his face young and anguished.

"I care about my job," she said impatiently, ignoring his hurt. She couldn't stop now. "I don't want to lose my job and my reputation. It's easy to do that, Jerry. I might not be able to get another teaching job anywhere."

"I'd look after you," he said eagerly. "We could get married."

"Married?" She stared, then laughed harshly. "My God, Jerry, I'm ten years older than you. Don't be silly."

He stood up slowly. "You're laughing at me. You don't really care about me."

She saw her mistake. "I'm laughing at the idea of our marriage, that's all. You must marry someone young, your own age, someone—"

"No. You don't mean that. You're through with me. You're tired of me. You're sick of me. That's what."

She set her lips. She had known this would be hard. "Jerry, try to understand. All the campus is talking. If this gets to the Board, I'll be fired. I took a chance in beginning this affair—"

"Affair—that's all it means to you. I love you. But to you it's just an affair. You don't care about me."

"Jerry—" She couldn't deny what he said. She did not love him. "I thought that was all it mean to you, also. An affair. A wonderful, foolish, lovely time—"

He would not listen. "You don't love me," he rasped, "you never did. You're a bitch—a bitch."

"Jerry—"

He backed to the door, looking awkward, terrible, accusing and pathetic as he repeated the word with intensity. "A bitch. That's all. You've never loved, you're a bitch. You just slept with me. You'll be sorry, I'll make you sorry. You let me make love to you—oh, God. Just a bitch." He turned and ran out and clattered down the steps, taking them two and three at a time. She heard the outer door bang a moment later.

She closed her apartment door, leaned against it limply. Jerry had called her a bitch. And he was right. That was what she was, that was how she had acted. She hadn't loved Jerry. She had wanted him, his long lean powerful body driving at her, his kisses, his caresses, his adoration.

Sorry? He would make her sorry?

"Oh, Jerry, I'm sorry already," she whispered. "Terribly sorry. I've hurt you. I never meant to hurt you. I only wanted the pleasure of love—no, the pleasure of sex. That was all. Oh, Jerry, I'm sorry."

He wasn't there to hear her. He was out somewhere in the darkness, running away like a hurt animal, trying to find a dark hole where he could hide until his wounds were healed.

His wounds would heal, she thought. He would recover. He would find some nice girl his own age and love her and give her all the overflowing adoration he had wanted to give Claire.

Claire couldn't help feeling relieved that the affair was kaput. She felt free again after the long months of being in willing bondage to a young demanding lover. She stretched out on the couch, weary, relaxing, thankful the relationship was finished. Jerry was a dear boy, but she was through with boys. They satisfied for a while, then they could no longer satisfy.

Her thoughts wandered to Wayne Kincaid. He was thoroughly masculine, demanding, aggravating, aggresive. He wanted to control her, not only her body, but her mind as well, and eventually win emotional control over her. She wasn't sure she wanted that.

Wayne. She lay still, her eyes closed, thinking of Wayne. She was free to think of him now. She would date him again, but would carefully avoid his apartment. She would not become involved in another affair so soon. She would wait and learn to know him and wait.

No more rushing into intimate relationships before she had counted the cost. It could hurt people, as she had hurt Jerry. She didn't want to hurt anyone like that again.

CHAPTER NINE

FRIDAY evening Elsie Zeck was sitting beside Jerry in his car as they rode swiftly to a motel he knew where they could be together.

Elsie was dazed, happy, incredulous. How had it happened? After all these months of trying vainly to attract Jerry's attention, she had succeeded. But how? She still didn't know.

She had been sitting in a booth at the drugstore with Dan on Thursday afternoon. Jerry had walked in, had sat down beside her. Right in front of Dan, Jerry had asked her for a date that evening. How Dan had scowled when she had accepted. Elsie giggled happily. That evening Jerry had kissed her until they had both wanted much more.

He had suggested a motel and maybe staying the weekend. She had accepted so quickly that they had both been surprised.

Why had he asked, after ignoring her all this time? she wondered. Oh, what did it matter? He had asked her. She would give him such a marvelous time that he would begin to love her.

It didn't take Jerry long to register them at the motel. It was the same one where she had gone with Dan, Elsie realized. Oh, well, that had been a good training experience.

Nothing had mattered when she was with Dan. She hadn't cared what he thought of her, just so the word would go around that Elsie Zeck was a real hot number, and that Jerry would hear the word.

Now she trembled and was unsure of herself. Jerry mattered too much. She wanted desperately to attract and keep him. She walked into the motel room ahead of him, glanced around uneasily. Jerry carried in the suitcases, set them down with a thump.

"I'll lock the car," he said. "Are you hungry?"

"Hungry? No," said Elsie. Who could think of food at a time like this?

Elsie put her suitcase on the rack and opened it. Should she put on a nightgown? Or would he prefer to undress her? What should she do? For the first time in months she felt panicky about being with a man. She wanted so desperately to please Jerry.

Jerry returned and locked the bedroom door. He looked so grim and serious that she felt strange. Wasn't he happy about this? What was wrong?

She began, timidly, "Jerry, should I—"

He stalked over to his suitcase, opened it, and took out a whiskey bottle. She watched, surprised, as he opened it and tilted it to his lips. He drank several swallows, capped the bottle and put it on the dresser.

She took off her coat and hung it in the closet. Out of the corner of her eye she saw Jerry undressing. So she took off her skirt and sweater and hung them up also. She waited for him to notice her in her thin red slip. He didn't even look at her. He was taking off his shoes.

She hesitated, then took off everything and slid into the wide bed. Jerry finished undressing, and stood naked in front of the dresser. He was so tall, so big, so much more a man than any of the boys she had dated. She felt pride and love—and fear that she could not please him.

She watched him as he opened the bottle again to drink several more long swallows. She hadn't known that Jerry drank so much. It was odd he could drink like that and still be such a good athlete. Or had he only started drinking recently?

He turned out the lights. She moved down under the covers, waiting. He came to bed. She felt the bed mattress yield under his weight, felt his warmth as he stretched out beside her.

He reached for her at once.

"Oh, Jerry, Jerry," she whispered tremulously. She had wanted him so long, had waited so long. She closed her arms convulsively around his big body. He was bending over her. He was kissing her throat, her shoulder, her breast.

Jerry was hungry. They dressed and ate in the motel dining room, careless of who might see them. Then they sauntered back to their room where they quickly undressed again.

Jerry had another long drink from the bottle. Then he slipped into bed where they lay and made love for long lazy hours.

They went back to school on Monday morning to find the campus in an uproar. It seemed that the parents of two students had stayed at the motel Sunday night and had seen Jerry and Elsie and had recognized them. They had notified the Dean.

The Dean called them to his office and asked if the report was true.

"Yes, it was," said Jerry, so casually that Elsie stared at him in astonishment. Didn't he care? she wondered. Did he love her so much that what other people said didn't matter?

The Dean gave them a long lecture. Jerry didn't seem to listen to it. Elsie decided she wouldn't mind, either. If Jerry loved her, nothing else mattered.

"If you were going steady—but you're not even dating regularly," said the Dean at last. His face was flushed and disturbed. "I can only conclude that you want to cause a scandal. Are you asking to be expelled?"

"Oh, no!" said Elsie, nervously. This was Jerry's senior year. "Of course not."

"Then why did you do it?"

Elsie glanced at Jerry. He didn't seem inclined to explain. "We love each other," she said.

"Love? But you're not engaged, are you?"

"Yes. Yes, we're engaged," said Elsie. "We're going to be married. After school is over, of course. After Jerry graduates."

Jerry still didn't say a word, staring at the floor and brooding about something. Elsie felt very edgy. Why didn't he say something? But he hadn't denied that they were in love and were going to be married. That was something.

The Dean dismissed them, saying he would see them again after he had talked to the President of the college.

The students became very upset when it was rumored Jerry Arnold might be dismissed from school. They held a rally and marched around that evening with banners and signs protesting Jerry's right to love a girl. Elsie felt very odd about that also. She hadn't counted on her love affair being known and discussed publicly by everybody.

But she seemed to be regarded as the heroine of a great romance, and she was treated with respect and admiration by the students, and with caution by the faculty. Even Professor Claire Frazier stared at her in class as though wondering what kind of a girl Elsie was. Now she didn't dare to scold Elsie, the green-eyed girl thought Elsie had shown her she could take Jerry away from Claire.

The Dean decided against dismissing the pair from school, and the campus calmed down. Jerry often asked Elsie out, and once they went back to the motel for a weekend. Jerry was very tender and kind this time, and he didn't have a bottle of whiskey with him. Elsie felt relieved about that

They did not discuss their so-called "engagement." Jerry didn't ask Elsie formally to marry him. But he wasn't dating anyone else, and she didn't date anyone else. She was very happy.

It seemed to take a long time for a girl to get what she wanted, Elsie thought. But if she tried and tried, it worked out So Elsie concluded, with great satisfaction.

Claire had been genuinely shocked by the motel episode. See couldn't help believing that she had driven Jerry to this, that it was his way of "making her sorry." Poor Elsie Zeck, Claire thought, her reputation was ruined now.

But, as the weeks passed, the teacher revised her opinions on the matter. Jerry and Elsie were engaged, they said. Elsie, in class, seemed in a daze of happiness. She glowed, she beamed, she laughed. Jerry didn't come near Claire.

Maybe this was just what Jerry had needed—a shove away from Claire toward a young attractive girl much closer his own age. Claire winced at first, but she came to see it as a good thing.

There was another positive element. Since Claire was free of Jerry, she was also free to think of Wayne Kincaid more seriously. Her previous two affairs had been with men much younger than herself. Wayne was different. She had been afraid of him, she admitted now.

Wayne barged into her classroom one afternoon a couple weeks after the Jerry-Elsie motel episode. He seemed to know just when to find her alone.

Claire stiffened warily. She never knew quite what to expect from him. He never bored her, as Jerry had. Wayne had a gift for the unexpected.

"Hi, Claire," he said cheerfully.

"Hello." He came over and sat on the edge of her desk, too close. She was intensely aware of his masculinity, his aggressive strength. He brushed the back of his hand swiftly against her cheek. She jerked away.

"I wanted to see if it was as soft as I remembered," he explained.

She knew she blushed, remembering the days and nights together when he had learned more of her than any man ever had.

"There's a concert Saturday evening in town," he said. "Symphony—all Brahms. How about it?"

She hesitated. She was hungry for good music, she liked being with Wayne, she was free of Jerry.

"All right," she said. "It sounds good." She smiled.

He seemed surprised. "What? No struggle? No terror? No panic? I must be progressing."

She made a face at him, deliberately. He bent forward, held her head firmly with a hand at her neck, and kissed her mouth with insistent lips.

"I've been wanting to do that," he said.

She pulled at his wrist until he let her go. "You're getting too fresh," she scolded. "Now go on, and let me alone. I have piles of work to do."

"So have I, but I have a much better idea about how to spend some time. Come on over to my apartment, and I'll show you what I mean."

"Ha," she said. "I suppose you want me to look at your etchings."

"We could start there, if you insist." His eyes were teasing, and eager.

She shook her head. "No, really. I do have work. All these papers to read." She riffled the pile on her desk.

He sighed. "You're too conscientious. I look at the girls in my classes and think—what good is education going to do these lovely things? All they have in their brains is a technique for chasing and getting their man. Then marriage and babies. What good is a college degree going to be to them?"

"Oh, really," Claire flared up at this age-old argument. "Even if all they ever do is take care of a husband and children, an education is important. A child's first teacher is his mother. Her attitudes, her beliefs, her prejudices or liberalisms give him indelible impressions. What worse start can a child have than education at the hands of an ignorant, superstitious, narrow-minded, frustrated woman?" She paused for breath.

"Go on, go on," he egged her on eagerly.

"Oh, you just want me to get angry."

He grinned. "I like to see you become excited," he admitted frankly.

"And besides," she could not help continuing, "women live a lot longer than men, and a lot longer than women used to. After their children are grown, what should they do? Play bridge all day? Or twiddle their thumbs in front of television? They have twenty or thirty or forty useful years. They can pick up where they left off, begin again in teaching, science, industry. America is not so wealthy in knowledge that it can afford to waste so many women and their potential."

"How would you like to give a speech at my next stag party, on the uses of women?" he teased.

She slapped at him. He caught her arm, kissed her hand swiftly.

"Don't be angry," he said more calmly. "I agree with you on this. I just wanted to hear what you had to say. And I like you when you're aroused."

She shook her head at him, freed her hand. "Some time, some day, I'll get so angry at you—" she threatened.

"Just so we're in bed at the time, sweet," he said, grinning. "I can manage you there."

She flushed hotly. "Will you get out? How can I get any work done?"

He arose reluctantly. "All right, all right. I'll pick you up at six, Saturday night. How about an Italian dinner?"

She hesitated. Wine was her weakness, and he knew it But she could not resist.

"All right. Six," she said.

"I'll see you then."

He strolled out. She had trouble concentrating on the papers to be graded. He was too attractive, and he knew her too well.

Saturday night he demonstrated all too readily how well he knew her. The dinner was ordered in advance, her favorite lasagna, steak and a chilled white wine. She listened to the concert afterwards in a haze of repletion, the wine warming her blood, tingling her brain.

It was close to midnight when he brought her back to her apartment. She knew what he was going to do. She snapped on a couple lights. He was locking the door after them.

"Do you want some coffee?" she suggested weakly. "Or some more wine? I have some, somewhere—"

He took her coat from her, flung it with his overcoat on the couch.

"No more delays, Claire," he said. "I've been wanting you much too long."

He drew her into his arms and his mouth crushed down on hers. She felt her body go limp as he pulled her closer, his warm strong limbs pressing urgently against hers. Her eyes closed. He held her head with the palm of his hand while he pressed her lips in long slow kisses that seemed to burn through her.

She made no protest as he drew her to the bedroom. He undressed her swiftly, flinging the clothes this way and that until she stood naked before him. Then he pulled the hairpins out of her blond hair and he untangled the tight bun, thrusting his fingers through her hair until it fell to her shoulders.

He put his hands on her arms, looked at her so long she felt strange. He had seen her before, looked at her, but never like this. It was as though he possessed her with his eyes and his mind before he pushed her gently back to lie on the bed.

She waited for him as he undressed. The lights were dim, but she could see him, his long lean body, the dark hair on him, his dark eyes, his dark face so serious and intent now. Then he came to her, and lay beside her.

"It's been so long," he muttered. "So very long, Claire. Darling."

She turned to him as he put his arms around her. They lay, kissing, their bodies moving restlessly, their legs entwining. She put her arm under his neck, caressing his hair, his shoulder, as he kissed her. His hand trailed slowly over her body, so sweetly familiar, the remembered way he had touched her. He moved slowly, deliberately. She wanted him soon. He was such a tease, she thought, making her wait when she wanted him. She pulled at his waist.

"Wayne, don't wait. Hurry."

He kissed her waist, his dark head moving against her white skin, nuzzling her warm overheated body. She wiggled with impatient desire.

"Wayne, please. I want you."

He laughed softly. He kissed her hips and thighs, his tongue flicking on her flesh. It was so delicious, so pleasing, she felt. But she wanted more of the rough heavy pleasure.

"Wayne. Darling, darling." She opened her arms, begging. "Do it, you devil. Please."

His mouth sought other places, kissed with maddening deliberation. She shivered heavily.

He lifted up at last and laid his body firmly on hers as she writhed helplessly. But it was what she wanted, his bigness filling her, his masculinity dominating her, his heaviness forcing her to submission. And, at last, she cried out, crumpled up, the waves beating her into a quivering jelly of helplessness as he himself dissolved into bliss ...

Later she vaguely recalled that Wayne rolled her under the covers, snapped off the lights in the apartment, then came back to bed with her. In spite of or because of his teasing, he was a wonderful lover, drawing out his caressing, building up her desires to fever pitch before releasing them in a shuddering climax of pleasure. He seemed to know her so thoroughly that he was aware of just when to be rough with her and when to drive on to the finish.

She slept for a while, then wakened to find him leaning over her, making love to her sleepy body, rubbing her thighs with his legs to rouse her. They both fell asleep much later that night, legs tangled, her head on his chest, exhausted from their love play.

About eleven the next morning, she wakened to find he had departed, leaving a note on the bedside table.

"Claire—You're so lovely I can hardly bear to leave you. But for the sake of my reputation, I'm sneaking out. See you again soon, sweet. I adore your long legs. Love—Wayne."

She leaned up in bed, read the note again, drawing the blankets around her naked shoulders. She was worn out. When he wanted a woman, he really wanted everything. She yawned, stretched, fell back on the pillows and went back to sleep...

Now that Jerry was gone, it seemed silly, she thought later, to deny Wayne. He was discreet, coming home with her at midnight after a date, leaving early in the morning before he could be seen. And he was such a marvelous knowledgeable lover, giving her as much or more pleasure as he obtained for himself. He seemed to find as much fun in making her respond to an embrace as extracting his own satisfaction and release.

He was not nearly so cynical as she had thought early in their acquaintance. He loved to tease. He would tickle her unexpectedly, just when she was relaxed in his arms. When she jumped and doubled up defensively, he would laugh and run his fingers down her spine to her hips until she tingled with desire.

He loved to force her off guard, arouse her so she had no defenses left, make her so hot she would have to take the offensive. He would prepare her for an embrace, then lie back, arms under his head, looking so innocent and sleepy, yawning. Claire would jump up on him, panting, angry, her hips desperately seeking his. Then he would chuckle, and she would have to go ahead, leaping on him, urgently seeking the object of her lust. Only at the last would he help, his rough hands pulling her down, his body lunging to complete the movements.

Much as he teased, however, he never denied her satisfaction. He was not sadistic. She had all she could take, all she ever dreamed of wanting. And when they were both satiated, they would lie together on the bed, close, and he would rub his cheek against hers, and whisper, "Happy, sweet? Want more?"

She would answer dreamily, "No more now. I'm happy." And they would drift off to sleep.

Sometimes they talked, their words incongruous with their actions. In the middle of an embrace they would argue lazily or heatedly about a faculty decision, a point in philosophy, the treatment of a student. He seemed to enjoy making her argue with him as he kissed her, as though it added spice to their caressing.

When she was apart from him, warning bells rang in her mind. She was beginning to like him too much. She depended too much on his skillful lovemaking, his satisfying embraces. He dominated her too easily now; she wanted him to do whatever he would with her. She found herself agreeing with his opinions in faculty meetings, and it was an effort for her to see the other side of questions.

If she didn't look out, he would have her completely under his spell. She was concerned about that. She never had wanted to be so dominated mentally. It was bad enough to undergo physical domination. Where was she drifting now?

She didn't want to stop. A week of classes would pass in a daze. Saturdays were for Wayne, with Wayne. She lived from weekend to weekend, feeling alive only when her lover held her in his arms. She didn't know where it would end. She couldn't believe it would ever end. She was blissfully, mindlessly, crazily happy.

CHAPTER TEN

WAYNE found he had been staring at a student's paper for half an hour without seeing it. He grunted, rose from his desk and walked out to the kitchen to make some coffee. He couldn't concentrate on grading papers. He couldn't get his mind away from Claire long enough to work.

He was in a pretty bad way, he bawled himself out. No other woman had ever attracted and interested him so much. She was terrific in every way, in and out of bed.

He made a pot of coffee, carried the pot and cup back to the living room and sat down at his desk again. He had to get these fool papers finished.

He was getting more and more deeply involved with Claire. He had thought he might get tired of her and want to break off. Instead he was seriously considering asking her to marry him.

"Slow down, boy," he warned himself, surprised and amused to find he was so deeply in love. "Don't jump into anything. You have waited this long to get married. Make sure she's the right one first."

But how could he make sure? He was fond of Claire, felt tender toward her, loved to tease her, liked her cooking, liked to go out with her, liked to argue with her and get her excited. And in bed—

"No complaints," he said dreamily, aloud, remembering the session last Saturday night. How she could love. And how adorable her lovely long body was, the soft big breasts, the firm thighs, every kissable place on her. He groaned, took another swallow of coffee. This wasn't accomplishing any work.

One thing bothered him. Well, two things really. First, he didn't kid himself that he had taught her all about sex. Who had been her first teacher? Second, where did Jerry Arnold fit into the picture? How deeply was Claire involved with the athletic hero? That scene at the dance had not been the result of a momentary one-sided crush. Claire had been thrown for a loop. She had not been able to manage the boy. And shortly thereafter there had been the scandal of Jerry and that young girl, their weekend at a motel. That had been an odd business. It had seemed that Jerry had made no effort to conceal his affair. What had he been trying to prove?

Maybe Claire was being square with Wayne, maybe not. She was usually so blunt and honest he would hate to think of her deceiving him.

Wayne watched her that week whenever he saw her. He was trying to make up his mind whether or not to propose. He sat behind her in faculty meeting, admiring the curve of her cheek, the prim upsweep of her blond hair, the small ear with the single pearl earring. All very modest, very demure, he thought. This for the public eye. His private vision saw her otherwise, begging him in passionate words to complete the embrace he had begun.

There was a faculty social one afternoon, tea and cakes. Ordinarily Wayne found them boring, and either avoided them or left early. This afternoon he watched Claire, watched the expert way she juggled several professors in conversation, managed a notorious gossipy wife, downed three cups of tea without eating any of the overly sweet cakes, smiled and remained bright-eyed through two hours of dull talk in a hot crowded room. Yes, as a faculty wife she would be a decided asset.

"... Jerry Arnold," Wayne heard a gossip say, with such happy accent that Wayne perked his ears for the comment to follow. "The Dean doesn't dare throw him out of school, or that girl either, what's her name?"

"Zeck, Elsie Zeck," someone supplied.

"Yes. Well, I heard that some alumni telephoned the Dean and said if he did anything to ruin the basketball team's chances for the trophy, they would act. And they meant it. Imagine, a campus like Dexter being intimidated by basketball fans. It's a disgrace," the gossip said happily. "Simply a disgrace."

"I can't imagine what we're coming to," agreed another woman. "Why, they don't even bother to cover up their activities! They go out openly, register at motels. In my day—"

Wayne drifted away as the conversation turned to the gossip's day, many years back. Obviously time had altered some facts and blurred others. Wayne seemed to recall that many years ago the gossip's husband had been involved with a fan dancer and had not bothered to conceal his activities any more than the fan had concealed the dancer's charms. Time does strange things to memories, he philosophized as he edged near enough to Claire to hear her voice.

They had a date again on Saturday evening to see a foreign film before it would be banned.

The film was rather innocuous except for a couple irrelevant over-publicized scenes. Claire and Wayne were disappointed. They strolled out arm-in-arm.

"I thought it would be a lot worse than that," sighed Claire.

"Too bad. If it isn't banned, no one will bother to try to see it."

"That love scene at the hotel," she said. "That was actually ridiculous. It was all suggestion. They didn't really do anything. They didn't have a chance."

"Poor kids," said Wayne. "We can do a lot better than that. Shall we go to your place or mine?"

"Mine," said Claire, without blushing. "I would never wake up in time to sneak out early, the way you do."

"It's more and more of an effort," he said. "I wake up, look at you sleeping away, and want to wake you up. But if I wake you, then you don't let me leave."

Now she blushed. "That's not true. That was your fault last week. You started kissing me—"

They argued amiably all the way back to her apartment. Once in bed, their arguments turned into a contest of skills in which both won and were highly content.

Wayne left early, as usual, but all Sunday morning he pondered. On Sunday afternoon he went back to her apartment and rang the bell. He waited a couple minutes, and rang again.

Someone padded near to the door and called, sleepily. "Who is it?"

"Wayne."

"Oh." Claire opened the door, holding it cautiously to herself. When he came in and shut the door he saw why. She was clad only in a thin pink negligeé and a pair of pink fuzzy slippers. He could see through the negligee to her loveliness, and it was very lovely indeed.

"Hi, darling," he said, and took her in his arms and kissed her. Her mouth was warm and sleepy, her body lax. "Have you been asleep all this time?"

"Of course. How else can I get through the week after a night of your brutal attacks?"

"Um," he said, tasting her soft cheek with his tongue. "Good."

She pulled away. "Now, don't start that. I haven't recovered from last night. Why did you come back?"

She could probably be persuaded to join him in bed for some more brutal attacks, but he meant to be serious. He drew her over to the couch and pulled her down to sit on his lap. Her soft weight made him regret his own resolve.

"I want to talk to you," he said.

She put her arm around his neck lazily, and tickled his ear. "Really?"

"Yes. Seriously."

She put her hand on his cheek, held it there while she looked straight into his eyes. He wanted to kiss her red full mouth, bury his head in the soft hollow between her breasts, put his hands under the thin film of pink that covered her legs. But he must be serious.

"All right, sweet. Seriously," she said.

"I've been thinking for some time that we get along quite well."

"Oh, quite," she cooed suggestively, tickling his ear some more. "We seem to fit together, don't you think?"

He was going to lose the thread of the logic completely if he weren't careful. He continued with a rush. "I'm more and more crazy about you. I—I love you, Claire. I think we could be terrifically happy together."

She sat still, her face serious all at once. "What do you mean? What do you want?"

"You," he said simply. "You, all the time. Marriage. Forever. Will you marry me, Claire?"

She was stunned, her emerald eyes flaring wide. "Marry?"

"Yes." Suddenly he was scared. What if she didn't want marriage? What if all she wanted was an affair? He broke out in a cold sweat, trembling. "Yes. I want you to marry me."

She was silent. She turned her face so it pressed against his shoulder. He couldn't see into her eyes, her tell-tale changeable eyes. Her hand was rigid on his neck.

He was in a panic. What was she thinking? What more could he say? He couldn't think of anything more. She knew him well by this time. What was she afraid of? Losing her independence? But that had to be in marriage. Each had to give up some freedom in order to achieve union. Was she such a tough bachelor girl she didn't want any part of a marriage union? He could not believe that.

She stirred. "Wayne," she said huskily.

"Yes?"

She turned her head. "Oh, Wayne. I want to, but I don't know. I'm not sure—"

"I think we would be good together, as good as we are in bed."

She was silent for a long minute. Then she sighed, a deep unconscious sigh. "All right."

"What?"

"All right. I will marry you. I want to."

He grabbed her tight and kissed her in a frenzy of relief. "Oh, honey, oh, sweet. You scared me to death."

Her arms closed tight around him. Her open mouth kissed his cheek as his hands shoved the pink silk aside recklessly. "Do—do you love me?" she whispered.

He remembered that women needed words. "I love you, Claire. I love you like crazy."

"I love you too. I love you."

He hugged her tight. He was about to pick her up and take her to the bedroom when he remembered one of his doubts. "Listen, Claire. Just one thing."

"Yes," she said softly.

"I've wondered. What was your relation to Jerry Arnold?"

He felt the jolt which that had given her. She stiffened. Her arms came down. "Jerry? What does he have to do with us?" She was angry, her cat's eyes flaring wide, yellowing near the pupils.

He watched her face. "I want to know, Claire. That scene at the dance, the way he kept coming back. That wasn't puppy love, was it?"

"What if it was or wasn't? What difference does it make?" She got off his knees, drew the thin robe about her and refastened the sash. He stood up.

He had to know, to have it out in the open. "Did you and Jerry Arnold have an affair?"

She gasped. He could feel she was going to lie to him. She faced him defiantly, her eyes glittering, her chin up. Then the glitter died.

"Yes. Yes, we did. But it's over."

He grew cold, then hot. He became so angry that it made him reckless. "Over? But you had an affair? You slept with him?"

"Yes."

"In your bed? In there?" He pointed to the bedroom, outraged and jealous.

"Yes."

"While you were going with me?" he demanded.

Her face was drained of color, her eyes huge, darker green. "Yes. But it's over, Wayne, it's over. He was only a boy."

"A boy. A pretty big boy," said Wayne, furious with jealousy. "Did he satisfy you too?" He caught her shoulders, shook her. "Did he satisfy you?"

"Yes. Physically."

He could have struck her. Wayne's woman, Wayne's mistress. And she had been seeing Jerry also. Jerry Arnold had seen the soft flesh crumpling under his body, had felt the delights of her swift reactions, had heard her voice moaning.

"You seem to like variety," Wayne heard his own voice say with cold clarity. "I'm sure I couldn't satisfy you all the time, if you like the boy type also. And I wouldn't want to share my wife."

"Wayne, don't say that. It's over—don't say that—"

He walked blindly to the door. He never wanted to see her again, never wanted to touch her soft flesh, to smell her perfumed sweetness, to kiss her till she crumpled up in helpless desire.

"Sorry I made a fool of myself," he said. "I shouldn't have bothered to propose. I imagine a woman like you wouldn't want marriage. It would be too confining. Goodbye."

"Wayne!"

He slammed the door, shutting off the sound of her cry. He ran down the steps as though tempting demons might follow him. He drove back to his apartment, and couldn't remember later where he had parked his car.

He was well rid of her, he reminded himself again and again the next weeks. She couldn't be trusted. A woman couldn't be trusted. Anyone that hungry for sex was no good. He should have suspected something was wrong.

But she was awfully good in bed, a demon whispered in his ear. Nothing wrong with the way she could make love.

She was no damn good, he answered himself. He was lucky he had found out what she was like. Carrying on an affair with a college boy, a mere boy.

But Jerry Arnold was a big and husky boy, quite a man in bed, the demon whispered.

Wayne writhed with jealous fury. Claire had slept some nights with him, some nights with Jerry. He had shared his love with a boy. How many others? How many others did Claire know?

He couldn't forget Claire. He saw her every day at school, on the campus, in the halls, in meetings, in town. He could not avoid her. And she looked more desirable than ever, now that he could not touch her nor go up to her apartment and lie in bed long hours with her.

He told himself she was a fever he would have to get over. But it wasn't easy. Not easy at all . . .

Claire missed Wayne more than she had ever dreamed she could miss anyone. His anger and desertion of her wakened her sharply to the realization of what she had been doing. Her affairs with Gino, Jerry and then Wayne had been selfish experiments in pleasure.

She had never tried to analyze her motives in this manner before. She had excused herself by saying that after all she was becoming older, that she was "free," that she had a right to do whatever she pleased so long as she hurt no one. Now she began to see that by using these "rights," she had hurt herself badly.

What if she had never carried on an affair? What if Wayne had simply come along, they had learned to know each other, they had fallen in love and they had decided to marry? Her record would have been clear. He could never have had grounds to accuse her as he had.

Yet—Claire frowned. She knew she had been morally wrong. Yet, what if Gino had never taught her about sex and love? What if she had still been inhibited by fear and frustration? Would Wayne have bothered to seek her out for dates? Would he have looked at her twice?

What if at Wayne's first advance she had frozen up and said, "Unhand me, villain," or whatever the modern equivalent expression might be. He would have walked out of her life without glancing back at her.

She drummed her fingers impatiently on the desk top. Life could be so unfair. The very affairs that had turned Wayne against her were the ones that had made her vulnerable to his attentions, had made her into the kind of woman he wanted.

She would not try to lure him back. He was a man. He knew what he wanted, or he should know by this time. If he couldn't take the good with the bad, so much the worse for him.

But all her rationalizations did not prevent her from missing him, their dates, their violent inconsequential arguments, his teasing, his exciting masculinity, their wonderful sessions in bed. She was not relieved to be rid of him as she had been with Jerry and Gino. She could not mull romantically over memories of Wayne, feeling a gentle pleasant nostalgia. It hurt her to think of him, hurt like a raw open wound that refused to heal.

Claire was glad to plunge into the heavy round of mid-term papers and examinations that led up to spring vacation. She drove her students and herself very hard, and overheard one student's complaint, "I thought you said Frazier's courses were snaps. I should have known better than to take your word."

"Well, she used to be easy," said the other girl.

There was nothing like hearing a frank appraisal. Claire grimaced. She had thought she was being fair and not too demanding in her subjects. Instead she had acquired the reputation for being easy.

Exams were finally terminated on Friday. Next would come nine days of vacation before school began again, before the exciting race began toward graduation and summer vacation. Claire left the college campus after her last class on Friday afternoon. Her portfolio bulged with essays, papers and examinations. They should keep her quite busy until school began again, she thought.

Back at her apartment she changed her clothes to her favorite grey slacks and white tee shirt. She brushed out her blond hair and left it in comfortable looseness over her shoulders. She put on anklets and moccasins. Nobody would be coming to see her. She would be completely comfortable for a change.

She decided to give herself the evening off before starting in to grade papers. She had a leisurely supper, reading an English journal between bites. After dishes were done, she piled records on the player and curled up on the couch to read more of the accumulated journals and magazines.

Her weariness, the lulling music and the effort of reading with tired eyes made her fall asleep. She wakened with a jerk. She had finally heard the doorbell ringing insistently.

She staggered to her feet, turned down the music and managed to reach the door as the bell rang again.

She opened the door and stared. "Jerry?"

He pushed past her and came in. He closed the door. "Hello, Claire," he said.

She looked stupidly at her watch. It was after ten o'clock. "Jerry, what are you doing here at this hour?"

"I came back," he said triumphantly.

"Huh?" She rubbed her head to clear it.

"I came back." He tried to take her in his arms. She yanked herself away. "I broke off with Elsie tonight. I don't love her. I told her so. I can't get you out of my mind."

"Oh, hell," moaned Claire. As though she didn't have enough trouble. "What did Elsie say?" If only Claire weren't so sleepy, if only she could think straight.

"Elsie? She doesn't matter." He grabbed her with powerful hands and shook her. "What's the matter with you? Don't you understand me?"

"Frankly, no. I've been asleep. I need some coffee." She seized on her own idea thankfully and headed for the kitchen. Blessed coffee.

Jerry followed her. "I don't get you, Claire. I know you've broken off with Professor Kincaid. And I was getting tired of Elsie. She's nothing but a kid. So I broke off with her, and now I'm back. Aren't you glad? What's wrong with you, anyway?"

Claire was too tired and sleepy to be tactful. "What's wrong is that I've grown up," she said testily. "I'm not in love with you. I don't know what you've heard about me and Wayne, but it's none of your damn business. And I'm not taking you back, so get that straight."

Jerry looked as though he had been yanked out of the game just as he expected to go over the goal line for a touchdown. "I don't get it. You—I love you. Don't you feel anything for me?"

"I liked you. You were a good lover," said Claire bluntly, she unplugged the coffee pot and set it on the table. "Cup of coffee?"

"Yeah. I guess so. Thanks."

They sat down and she poured the cups. She couldn't remember if he used cream or sugar. The affair with Jerry seemed a long time ago.

The coffee wakened her. "Now, let me get this," Claire said, after her cup was empty. "You were engaged to Elsie."

"Yes. I guess. She thought so anyway."

"And she's a sweet, sensitive, shy kid who doesn't know the score. So what did you tell her?"

Jerry began to look uneasy. "Well, Elsie wanted to set the wedding date. We've been going out a lot."

"You've been having a very obvious well-publicized affair, you mean. The whole campus knew it every time you climbed in bed with her."

Jerry turned red. His legs shifted awkwardly under the small table. "It wasn't that bad. We were just having fun."

"A girl like Elsie doesn't allow a guy like you to wreck her reputation for fun. She must be completely crazy about you."

Jerry stared at her. "You think so? Really? She said she loved me, but I didn't think she really meant it, because I didn't mean it either."

Men. How impossible they were, Claire thought

"So what did you tell her this evening?" she said.

"I was tired of her nagging at me to set the wedding date. I told her I didn't want to get married. I told her I was tired of her. I told her I was going to back to you."

"Great. Thanks so much to the boost you gave to my reputation," she said bitterly.

"She won't talk. She's a swell kid, really she is. If she was a little older, like you, she would be great."

"Time will remedy that, I feel certain." Claire was beginning to be very concerned about Elsie. It was evident to everyone except Jerry that the girl was madly in love with him. This must have been a crushing blow to her. She had ruined her reputation, thrown herself at Jerry, risked her college record, her parents' anger, all to have Jerry give her the brush. What would happen to a sensitive girl like Elsie? What would Claire do if she were in Elsie's place?

That thought was no help. The two females were utterly unlike.

"I'd better talk to Elsie," said Claire. She looked at her watch. Almost eleven. "It's too late to call her at the dorm. I hope she won't try anything drastic."

"Drastic? What?"

"Like suicide," said Claire sharply. "It has happened. Elsie is a very sensitive girl. She is likely to go off on some wild tangent. Do you think she seemed very upset tonight?"

"I don't know. No, she seemed very calm. Very," said Jerry, frowning. "At least, I think so. You don't think she would commit suicide, do you?"

"She might. But if she were calm— Well, I'll wait till morning," said Claire, reluctant to start out tonight. She was so tired and sleepy. "I'll see her tomorrow and have a talk with her and try to judge how upset she is. You might have been kinder to her."

"Is there any kind way to tell someone you don't love them and want to break off with them?" said Jerry.

Claire thought of Wayne. "No, I guess not," she said. "I guess not."

"Could I stay tonight with you?" said Jerry.

Claire gathered up the cups. "Stay?" she questioned, her mind still with Wayne. "What do you mean?"

He came up behind her and put his hands on her waist. "I mean, stay with you. Make love. I've missed you so much, Claire. Sweet," he whispered, and kissed the back of her neck.

She stiffened. "Let me go. That's over," she said. She wasn't even angry, only indifferent. "I don't love you. I still love Wayne, whether he cares for me or not. I don't want any other man to touch me."

He let her go. "You can say it. I guess you're tougher than me. You can say right out that you don't love me."

She turned around. "I'm sorry, Jerry. I was wrong ever to start an affair with you. We both got hurt, in different ways. But it won't help to begin an affair all over again. We're finished, through."

He accepted that and departed. She worried for a while about Elsie, but decided to wait until morning to call the dorm.

She called about ten in the morning. Elsie's roommate came to the telephone.

"Oh, Miss Frazier, I'm so scared about Elsie," said Harriet. She was crying.

"Scared? Why? How is she?"

"She's gone. She came in about nine after a date with Jerry. She was queer, laughing and saying nothing matters in the world and why shouldn't she do whatever she pleases. And she said she was going to Lake Helen."

"Lake Helen? Oh, good grief—"

"A whole bunch of kids have gone there. All the wild ones who went last year. I'm afraid—" She lowered her voice to a piercing whisper. "I'm afraid it's sex parties. Real orgies, you know. Oh, she has changed so much this year."

"Did she take a suitcase?"

"Yes. Some slacks and sweaters. And, oh yes, a blanket. She said she was going to sleep on the beach."

"Did you tell the Dean?"

"No. I was afraid she would get expelled."

"All right. I'm going after her. Don't worry now."

Claire hung up, and then called Jerry. He was at the frat house.

"Elsie has gone to Lake Helen with some of the students," she told him crisply. "I'm going after her. There's no telling what trouble she could get into."

"I never realized she—I'd better go. Listen, I'll go after her. She's my responsibility."

"I'm glad you realize that. But I had better go too. Why don't we both go? I don't have a car. How far is it?"

"About sixty miles. She might be hard to find. It's a big place, they tell me."

"I'll take a suitcase and a couple blankets in case we have to stay. Pick me up in an hour."

"Okay, Miss Frazier."

After she had hung up, she realized he had spoken respectfully to her, as to a teacher. Just as well, she thought.

She was waiting at the apartment building door with her suitcase and blankets when Jerry drove up. She ran out and got in the car. She saw several students watching them as she got in, but she couldn't have cared less.

"Do you know how to get there?" she asked.

"Yeah. One of the fellows who went last Spring vacation told me, and marked the map for me."

"That's good." Jerry started the car with a jerk. His face was drawn and anxious.

"I never realized she would do anything like this. Do you think it's because of what I said to her?"

"Of course it is," said Claire.

"Jesus. They have a real wild time. Ted says they sleep together on the beach, and some fellows have cottages and have strip parties. Lots more fellows are there than girls, he said. And the girls are usually pretty tough ones."

Claire was silent. She couldn't help believing all this was directly her fault. If only they were in time, and could rescue Elsie before she went too far.

CHAPTER ELEVEN

CLAIRE and Jerry arrived at Lake Helen about one in the afternoon. Claire gasped as she saw the small town, the lake front, the beaches swarming with students. Cars were everywhere, from jalopies to late-model convertibles.

Most of the students were men, but there were many girls among them. It seemed a hopeless task to find Elsie, but Claire and Jerry had to begin somewhere.

"At least she's with some Dexter guys," Jerry said. "They ought to be easy to spot since I know them."

They drove slowly along the main street of the student-clogged town, watching for a familiar face. They recognized no one. Some of the students looked older and very tough. Claire thought of Elsie among them and felt a cold chill. That naive girl, whatever her recent experiences had been, would not have a chance among these hard cases.

"Some of those guys look like dopes," said Jerry.

Claire realized with a jolt that he meant dope addicts. "Poor Elsie," she muttered. "Turn down that street, Jerry. There are some kids in the park over there."

They drove past the park, slowly, searching anxiously. But there was no sign of Elsie, no sign of the fellows from Dexter. They searched for several hours through the town, first in the car, later on foot. No trace.

"Let me call the college dorm," Clarie finally suggested. "I'll talk to Harriet, Elsie's roommate. Maybe Elsie came back, or maybe she didn't come here at all. She might have gone home to her parents."

"That's a thought," Jerry agreed. He spotted Lake Helen's one and only decent restaurant with a readiness that suggested he had noticed it before. Claire was becoming hungry herself.

They parked the car and went in. The restaurant was jammed. Claire found a phone booth and closed herself in to shut out the noise and confusion, while Jerry tried to bribe up a table.

Harriet came to the phone but told Claire that Elsie had not returned. "And I talked to some fellows who went up last night," Harriet added. "They decided to come back today, but Elsie wouldn't come. She's with some other guys, they said. Some fellow promised to drive her back when she was ready."

In the hot stuffy phone booth, Claire shivered. Oh, the crazy lost child, she thought. Elsie would have no idea of what she was doing. Even Harriet seemed to have no conception of the trouble Elsie was in.

Claire hung up and opened the booth door. Jerry had managed to obtain a table. She pushed her way through the mob of students. Many of the men turned to stare and to whistle at her.

"Any luck?" said Jerry eagerly.

Claire shook her head. "No. She hasn't returned. But, Jerry, the other guys came back to the campus and left Elsie here. She joined another bunch of fellows and stayed."

"Oh, no!" Jerry exclaimed, apparently genuinely concerned and shocked. "She's in real trouble. We've got to find her."

A waitress fought her way through the mob to them. "What's yours?" she snapped, pushing back a lock of hair from her red cheeks.

"We had better eat. Maybe our last chance for a while," Claire suggested.

"Okay."

They ordered almost fast enough to satisfy the harried waitress who disappeared again into the crowd.

They ate. Claire scarcely tasted the food, worrying about Elsie. What if they couldn't find her? Were there any police in town? Could they help anyway?

"Claire," a voice exclaimed.

She jumped at the sound of the angry voice in her ear. She stared in dumb amazement at Wayne's face.

"You fool, you utter idiot." He said, "Half the campus saw you leave with Jerry. Haven't you got a brain in that silly head?"

She began to cough. Wayne pounded her back, still bawling her out. "You talk about your reputation, then you throw it out the window over a boy half your age."

"I'm not half her age," Jerry protested.

Claire, her eyes watering as she coughed and choked, tried to defend herself. "Didn't—come here—Elsie—have to find—"

"What? Don't try to talk. I'm taking you back to Dexter while there's still a chance."

"Listen," said Jerry. "We've got to find Elsie."

"Huh?" Wayne looked at him. "What?"

"Elsie," said Jerry. "Elsie Zeck. She came up here. We came to find her."

"Oh," said Wayne.

Claire relaxed and stopped trying to talk. Jerry had for once said the right thing.

Wayne pushed her over on the bench and crowded into the small booth with them. "You mean you didn't come up here to—I mean, you're looking for someone?"

"Elsie. Elsie Zeck," Jerry explained again patiently. "We're engaged, Elsie and I. But we had a quarrel and she came up here last night with some guys from Dexter. Now we found out the guys went home, but Elsie's still here. We have to find her. Some of these guys are no damn good. They'll half kill her."

"I see," said Wayne. His hand squeezed Claire's arm savagely in his relief, but she welcomed the pain. He had come after her. He did love her, or he wouldn't have been so jealous and have followed her. "Where have you been looking?" Wayne demanded.

"Everywhere," said Jerry. "In town, in the park, along the beaches. Of course, I was trying to spot the Dexter guys and their cars. We didn't find out till a few minutes ago that they had left Elsie."

They discussed several possibilities, including notifying the police.

"They would have the same trouble finding her that we have," said Jerry. "And more—because they don't know what she looks like."

They finally decided to keep on searching on their own. After Wayne had had a sandwich, they started out again.

They searched by car and then on foot along the beaches until long past midnight. There was no sign of Elsie. They did run across some fellows Jerry knew from another college. Jerry told them they were looking for a girl.

"She might be over at the cottages," one of the men suggested.

"Cottages? Where?" asked Wayne.

"There's a big bunch of cottages along the upper beaches across the lake. The guys who have money and get here first rent them and really live it up. They usually latch on to the prettiest girls."

Jerry drove them over to the other beach and they rode back and forth futilely. The cottages were lighted. Music and laughter and screaming echoed from the open doors and windows. But there was no way to find Elsie there except by breaking into one after the other.

"We've checked the other beaches pretty thoroughly," said Wayne. "My guess is that she is here. Why don't we grab some sleep and wait around till morning? She'll surely come out then."

Jerry wanted to keep looking, but Claire was worn to the bone. She got out the blankets she had brought along. They spread them out on the beach near a shack that afforded them some shelter from the rising night wind.

Claire took off her shoes and rolled herself up in a blanket. The sand seemed soft at first to her weary body and she was ready to sleep. A shriek of laughter came from a nearby cottage, and she was wide awake again. She tossed and turned.

Jerry was already asleep on one side of her, his boyish face turned up to the sky. Wayne, on her other side, put out his hand and touched her arm.

"Claire?"

"Yes," she murmured.

"I'm sorry. I shouldn't have thought you would do that. Your affair with Jerry is over, isn't it?"

"Yes. Over."

"Good." His hand stroked down her arm to find her hand. He clasped it warmly in his. "I missed you."

"I missed you, too."

"Couldn't get you out of my mind."

"Me, too," she said. Tears came to her eyes.

"I love you," he said.

"I love you."

"We'll talk tomorrow. Get some sleep," he said.

"All right. Good night."

"Good night, sweet."

She drifted off to sleep, her hand clasped in his, the sound of the lake rumbling softly in her ears.

She wakened at dawn, feeling rumpled, cross, sleepy, yet strangely content. Wayne had come back to her.

Jerry was up already, walking along the beach, throwing pebbles into the water with restless force. Wayne wakened when she stood up.

They conferred about what they should do. All they could think of was to walk up and down along the cottages and wait for people to come out. So they did, walking slowly, looking, searching the faces of sleepy students stumbling along the beach.

Farther up the beach were rows and rows of students sleeping, rolled in blankets. Empty beer cans lined their improvised beds. Claire glanced at the face of every girl. The girls seemed so young, so sweetly innocent as they lay sleeping, often between two fellows, who held them possessively even in sleep.

Claire, Wayne and Jerry walked the length of the north beach, then turned and walked back again. The sun rose higher in the sky, glittering on the waters of the smooth lake. A few early motorboats churned water as they roared across the lake and roared back again.

The trio became tired, hungry, exasperated. It seemed a futile search for a girl who didn't want to be found.

"I'll paddle her good when I get her," Jerry said wearily. "I'll paddle her so hard she won't stand up or sit down for a week."

Both men had stubbles of beard, and their clothes were mussed from sleeping in them.

"Maybe we had better call the police now," suggested Claire. "They could search the cottages."

"There would be legal problems," said Wayne. "No, our best bet is to keep going, keep looking."

The trio reached the end of the beach again and started back once more. Then Jerry gave a shout, and ran, racing to catch up with a girl who was stumbling along the road away from the beach.

"Elsie," he yelled.

She turned, glanced around uncertainly, then began to run away. A man came out of the cottage she had left, and ran after them.

"Trouble," said Claire, and ran also, Wayne with her. They caught up with the trio as the man struck Jerry, who had grabbed Elsie.

"Let her go," the man said. "She's my girl."

"No, I'm not," Elsie said, panting. Her clothes were ripped, there was a dark bruise on her cheek, a bloody scratch on her forehead. Her beautiful green eyes were dazed and wild.

The strange man grabbed her brutally and pulled. She gave a frightened cry. Jerry lunged at the man, his face contorted with rage. Jerry struck, knocked him down, was on him, beating at him.

Elsie shrank away from them, her face haunted. Claire caught her as she turned to run. "It's all right, Elsie," Claire said, "we'll help—don't run. We'll help you."

The girl stared at her, distraught. "But Jerry—Jerry said—" She began to cry.

"It's all right. It's all right," Claire soothed her, patting her shoulders.

Wayne was pulling Jerry off the other man. "Okay. You made your point. Let's not be murderous about it"

The man was so drunk he couldn't get up anyway. They left him lying on the sand and they concentrated on getting Elsie back to the car.

She fought them at first. "No, no, I won't go back. I'll stay if I want"

"With those guys?" asked Wayne, in weary amazement.

Jerry showed new maturity and understanding. "Elsie, I love you. I really do. I didn't mean what I said the other day."

"Yes, you did, you did!" she shouted. But she had stopped fighting him.

"I didn't mean it," he said, "I love you. I want to marry you. We'll get married right after graduation." His arm was around her, helping her to walk. Wayne and Claire dropped back tactfully to let them talk it out

By the time they had reached the car, Elsie had stopped crying. Jerry said, "I'll drive Elsie back to Dexter. We have things to talk over."

"I'll drive Claire then," Wayne agreed promptly. "Just let us off at the restaurant."

Jerry drove them back to the restaurant. When he and Elsie left, Elsie's mussed black curly hair was resting on Jerry's shoulder, and the two together took up little more than half of the front seat.

"I wonder," mused Wayne, as he unlocked his car, "if Jerry will remember to give her a paddling?"

Claire smiled. "Would you?"

They got in the car. Wayne leaned over and kissed her cheek. "I should paddle you. I would if I weren't so tired."

"I'm beat," she sighed. She went to sleep on the way back to town. Wayne wakened her at her apartment.

"I'd come up, but you're too tired to appreciate me," he said tenderly.

"Call me tomorrow," she said. He carried her suitcase up the steps, unlocked her door and put her inside.

She closed the door after he left and she staggered to bed. She didn't remember anything else until evening.

She got up, showered, had some supper and went back to bed. She had never wanted sleep so much in her life ...

Wayne phoned Claire at noon the next day, and dropped in about two o'clock. He looked at her with his familiar teasing look and said, "Let's go out for a walk."

"A walk?" said Claire, who had been expecting a different suggestion. "Why?"

"Because I want to talk to you. If we stay here, I won't get any talking done."

She put on her short red jacket and tied a red scarf over her blond hair. The March winds had not yet given way to gentle April breezes.

Outdoors it was chilly, but a warm sun made reckless promises to the trees and grass.

"Oh, it's beginning to feel like spring," said Claire.

They walked automatically in the direction of the campus and strolled along the sunny lanes back of the buildings. The campus was quiet, as most of the students had left for vacation.

Wayne began abruptly, "I admit I was very jealous of Jerry. But that's over, isn't it?"

"Yes. Quite over," said Claire.

"You should never have become involved with him," he said sternly.

Claire didn't want to spoil everything with a quarrel. Yet she wanted Wayne to realize why she had had the affair.

"Will you listen while I explain?" she asked. "You won't like it, but it has happened, and I want you to know why."

"All right," he said. He stuck his hands in his pockets as they strolled along.

Claire plunged in. "You see, last winter I had a sabbatical leave and went to Italy. I had never had an affair in my life. I had never even been very serious about any man. Then there were all those romantic artists and writers, going around arm in arm and sleeping together. No one seemed to think it was wrong. It seemed natural."

She paused, and looked at him sidewise. She couldn't read his expression.

"In fact," she went on, fumbling for her thoughts, "it seemed unnatural for me to be as I was—frustrated, alone, fearful. I felt all stiff and dried up, old inside. I had a birthday. Becoming thirty is sort of a big jolt, you know. Thirty always seems so old. Then you hit it yourself, and suddenly, bang, you're in the older class of citizens."

"I know. America makes a fetish of being young. Yet we live longer and longer. Thirty is not very far along in years, not any more."

"Yes. But I felt old. And alone. And wanting to experience life and love, even in a pretend way. Even though I didn't really love, I wanted to know what it was like to love."

"So you had an affair."

"With Gino. An Italian boy. He was years younger."

"What were you afraid of?"

She struggled with the last remnants of pride and distrust, and conquered them. "Of men. Of myself. Of being dominated," she said honestly. "I had been on my own for years. I didn't really want to fall in love. Falling in love seemed too much of a surrendering of myself. I wanted to experience love—in a detached way, not running the risk of getting hurt."

He put his hand in her arm and drew her close to walk in step. "So that explains you," he said. "And Jerry. He was just a continuation of Gino?"

"Yes. Until you came along. Then I got all mixed up."

"I suppose my motives weren't of the best," he admitted after a pause. "I saw you, wanted you, and after I found out how wonderful a mistress you were all I could think of was how to get you again." She felt a little chilled. Was that still the way he thought of her? "And my past is not lily-white," he added.

"I didn't think I was the first woman in your life," said Claire. "You learn fast, but not that fast."

"It looks like we both have some forgetting to do," said Wayne. "Why don't we let bygones be bygones and begin right here? I don't want to start over. All that courting to do. I just want to marry you and go on from there."

She was so relieved she felt giddy. "Marry?" she said hopefully.

"Yes. I thought we could be married in a couple days."

"Oh, no, I couldn't. I've got things to do," she said in a panic. It was all right to think of marriage in some abstract time, farther down the calendar. But not so suddenly. Not so fast. Giving up her freedom all at once.

"I hope you realize, dear Professor Frazier, that the campus has not been blind to the events of the past weeks? If we announce our engagement, what kind of talk, giggles, horseplay, et cetera, et cetera, will we have to take from the students as well as our revered colleagues?"

"Ugh, I hadn't thought of that."

"You may also recall what happened to Professor Linden and his fianceé last fall. And she was a student, not a teacher."

"Ugh. Double ugh."

"So I think it would be best to jump into matrimony with both feet, keeping eyes shut, before we are discovered. Are you afraid of me, Claire?"

She squeezed the hand that held her arm. "A little," she said unsteadily.

He smiled down at her. "The longer you think about it, the worse it will be. Anticipation is usually either lots better or lots worse than realization."

They talked a while longer as they meandered back and forth over the sunny sidewalks and paths of the quiet campus. The trees were beginning to bud, the grass was tinged with green. A few crocuses held up orange heads to challenge the sun.

Claire finally agreed to take the plunge and they decided to obtain the marriage license the next day. They returned to Claire's apartment and had supper, talking over plans.

Wayne said, "I'd rather move into your apartment and give up mine. Your bed is more comfortable. Then this summer we can look for a house."

"Do you want to stay on at Dexter?" she asked. "Are you satisfied with the teaching job here?"

"Yes. I like it. And Professor Neal has about decided to turn over the advanced psychology courses to me so he can concentrate on philosophy."

"Oh, that's wonderful."

"Do you want to go on teaching until you have a baby?" he asked bluntly.

"Yes, I think so. Maybe that won't be long though. If we're going to have a family, we had better start soon."

"I approve," said Wayne. "I figure having a family is the best way of curing a bachelor girl of her restlessness."

"Oh, you do," she exclaimed prettily. Their hands met on the table, clasped tightly.

They headed for bed soon after. As Wayne said, they had managed to stay out of bed long enough to test their willpower. Now they deserved a reward.

Wayne insisted on undressing her, brushing aside her weak rebuffs. "You undress and dress yourself every day," he said. "Why not let me have a turn?"

He enjoyed every moment of anticipation, she realized, as he removed each garment and then had her stand nude before him while he contemplated her. He told her to turn around slowly. She did, turning for his absorbed attention while she still felt embarrassed, as often as he had seen her.

He smacked her bottom lightly. "Okay, sweet, hop in."

As she climbed into bed obediently, she knew her independent days were at an end. Wayne meant to be boss, and she wouldn't have much to say about that

But there were compensations. When he took her in his arms, she had a wonderful feeling of security and contentment accompanying the excitement of the embrace. Now she wanted to be tightly, warmly involved with him, to make up for the weeks of separation.

He begin to kiss her breasts, holding one firmly in his hand. He flicked his tongue over the nipple until it stood up hard and taut. She felt her breasts burgeoning.

She moved restlessly. "Wayne," she whispered. "Take me now. Please."

"You'll have to wait," he told her. "I'm enjoying this. The hotter you are, the sweeter you are."

He knew her too well, she admitted to herself. The longer the embrace was protracted, the less she could control herself. Then he kissed her waist. She stiffened as he sank lower, relentlessly.

Heat swept through her body. She twisted in an effort to evade him. "Not like that," she protested. "Please finish. Please take me now."

But he made her wait longer, teasing her. Hot spasms flashed through her. She jerked under his ruthless hands. Her hips churned impatiently.

Then he came up to lie on her, his heavy body crushing her with delicious force. She groaned with delight as she received what she desired in full measure.

Then waves of passion rose and broke and fell upon them. She gripped his body with wet hands, crying out incoherently in her frenzy. He forced her to roll across the bed with him in the last waves of desire. Her legs gripped him frantically to hold him, until their last quivers of ecstasy had subsided …

When she recovered, he was drawing the sheet and blankets up over them. She curled herself up against his warm body and he held her close.

"You know, sweet, we had better get married this week," he said.

"We had better," she agreed, wearily satisfied. "Or people will count the months on their fingers."

He chuckled softly at her ear. A thrill shot down her spine. She closed her eyes, determined to sleep. She was so tired, so contented.

Then she felt him at her again, his hands stroking her suggestively. Not again, she thought Not so soon. How was she going to control him?

She couldn't. He was more than she could handle. He was going to do the controlling. She might as well make up her mind to that, she mused as she adjusted her body to his.

She had feared a man's domination; but it had happened. Wayne was dominating her physically, mentally, emotionally.

And she had a strong feeling she was going to love him all the more for it

THE END

www.ingramcontent.com/pod-product-compliance
Lightning Source LLC
Chambersburg PA
CBHW030349180626
46812CB00007B/2820